Murray Leinster, whose real name was William Fitzgerald Jenkins, was born in 1896 and published his first SF story in 1919. The prolific Mr. Leinster went on to write more than 35 science fiction novels and many stories. In 1956 he won the Hugo Award for the novelette *Exploration Team*, which eventually became one episode of the book *Colonial Survey*. *Time* magazine has called him the "Dean of modern science fiction." He died in 1975.

THE FORGOTTEN PLANET

MURRAY LEINSTER

Carroll & Graf Publishers, Inc.
New York

First Carroll & Graf edition 1990

Published by arrangement with Scott Meredith Literary
Agency, Inc.

The Forgotten Planet is based upon the *Mad Planet and Red
Dust* (copyrighted Amazing Stories 1926, 1927) and *Nightmare
Planet* (copyrighted 1953 by Gernsback Publications Inc.)

Carroll & Graf Publishers, Inc.
260 Fifth Avenue
New York, NY 10001

ISBN: 0-88184-616-3

Manufactured in the United States of America

To Joan Patricia Jenkins

Contents

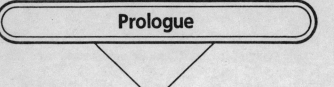

Prologue

THE SURVEY-SHIP *TETHYS* made the first landing on the planet, which had no name. It was an admirable planet in many ways. It had an ample atmosphere and many seas, which the nearby sun warmed so lavishly that a perpetual cloudbank hid them and most of the solid ground from view. It had mountains and continents and islands and high plateaus. It had day and night and wind and rain, and its mean temperature was within the range to which human beings could readily accommodate. It was rather on the tropic side, but not unpleasant.

But there was no life on it.

No animals roamed its continents. No vegetation grew from its rocks. Not even bacteria struggled with its stones to turn them into soil. So there was no soil. Rock and stones and gravel and even sand—yes. But no soil in which any vegetation could grow. No living thing, however small, swam in its oceans, so there was not even mud on its ocean-bottoms. It was one of that disappointing vast majority of

1

worlds which turned up when the Galaxy was first explored. People couldn't live on it because nothing had lived there before.

Its water was fresh and its oceans were harmless. Its air was germ-free and breathable. But it was of no use whatever for men. The only possible purpose it could serve would have been as a biological laboratory for experiments involving things growing in a germ-free environment. But there were too many planets like that already. When men first traveled to the stars they made the journey because it was starkly necessary to find new worlds for men to live on. Earth was over-crowded—terribly so. So men looked for new worlds to move to. They found plenty of new worlds, but presently they were searching desperately for new worlds where life had preceded them. It didn't matter whether the life was meek and harmless, or ferocious and deadly. If life of any sort were present, human beings could move in. But highly organized beings like men could not live where there was no other life.

So the Survey-Ship *Tethys* made sure that the world had no life upon it. Then it made routine measurements of the gravitational constant and the magnetic field and the temperature gradient; it took samples of the air and water. But that was all. The rocks were familiar enough. No novelties there! But the planet was simply useless. The survey-ship put its findings on a punched card, six inches by eight, and went hastily on in search of something better. The ship did not even open one of its ports while on the planet. There were no consequences of the *Tethys'* visit except that card. None whatever.

No other ship came near the planet for eight hundred years.

Nearly a millenium later, however, the Seed-Ship *Orana* arrived. By that time humanity had spread very widely and very far. There were colonies not less than a quarter of the way to the Galaxy's rim, and Earth was no longer over-crowded. There was still emigration, but it was now a trickle instead of the swarming flood of centuries before. Some of the first-colonized worlds had emigrants, now. Mankind did not want to crowd itself together again! Men now considered that there was no excuse for such monstrous slums as overcrowding produced.

Now, too, the star-ships were faster. A hundred light-years was a short journey. A thousand was not impractical. Explorers had gone many times farther, and reported worlds still waiting for mankind on beyond. But still the great majority of discovered planets did not contain life. Whole solar systems floated in space with no single living cell on any of their members.

So the Seed-Ships came into being. Theirs was not a glamorous service. They merely methodically contaminated the sterile worlds with life. The Seed-Ship *Orana* landed on this planet—which still had no name. It carefully infected it. It circled endlessly above the clouds, dribbling out a fine dust—the spores of every conceivable microörganism which could break down rock to powder, and turn that dust to soil. It was also a seeding of moulds and fungi and lichens, and everything which could turn powdery primitive soil into stuff on which higher forms of life could grow. The *Orana* polluted the seas with plankton. Then it, too, went away.

More centuries passed. Human ships again improved. A thousand light-years became a short journey. Explorers reached the Galaxy's very edge, and looked estimatingly across the emptiness toward other island universes. There were colonies in the Milky Way. There were freight-lines between star-clusters, and the commercial center of human affairs shifted some hundreds of parsecs toward the Rim. There were many worlds where the schools painstakingly taught the children what Earth was, and where, and that all other worlds had been populated from it. And the schools repeated, too, the one lesson that humankind seemed genuinely to have learned. That the secret of peace is freedom, and the secret of freedom is to be able to move away from people with whom you do not agree. There were no crowded worlds any more. But human beings love children, and they have them. And children grow up and need room. So more worlds had to be looked out for. They weren't urgently needed yet, but they would be.

Therefore, nearly a thousand years after the *Orana*, the Ecology-Ship *Ludred* swam to the planet from space and landed on it. It was a gigantic ship of highly improbable purpose. First of all, it checked on the consequences of the *Orana*'s visit.

They were highly satisfactory, from a technical point of view. Now there was soil which swarmed with minute living things. There were fungi which throve monstrously. The seas stank of minuscule life-forms. There were even some novelties, developed by the strictly local conditions. There were, for example, paramoecia as big as grapes, and yeasts had increased in size until they bore flowers visible to the naked eye. The life on the planet was not aboriginal, though. All of it was descended and adapted and modified from the microörganisms planted by the seed-ship whose hulk was long since rust, and whose crew were merely names in genealogies—if that.

The *Ludred* stayed on the planet a considerably longer time than either of the ships that had visited it before. It dropped the seeds of plants. It broadcast innumerable varieties of things which should take root and grow. In some places it deliberately seeded the stinking soil. It put marine plants in the oceans. It put alpine plants on the high ground. And when all its stable varieties were set out it added plants which were genetically unstable. For generations to come they would throw sports, some of which should be especially suited to this planetary environment.

Before it left, the *Ludred* dumped finny fish into the seas. At first they would live on the plankton which made the oceans almost broth. There were many varieties of fish. Some would multiply swiftly while small; others would grow and feed on the smaller varieties. And as a last activity, the *Ludred* set up refrigeration-units loaded with insect-eggs. Some would release their contents as soon as plants had grown enough to furnish them with food. Others would allow their contents to hatch only after certain other varieties had multiplied—to be their food-supply.

When the Ecology-Ship left, it had done a very painstaking job. It had treated the planet to a sort of Russell's Mixture of life-forms. The real Russell's Mixture is that blend of the simple elements in the proportions found in suns. This was a blend of life-forms in which some should survive by consuming the now-habituated flora, others by preying on the former. The planet was stocked, in effect, with everything that it could be hoped would live there.

But only certain things could have that hope. Nothing which needed parental care had any chance of survival. The creatures seeded at this time had to be those which could care for themselves from the instant they burst their eggs. So there were no birds or mammals. Trees and plants of many kinds, fish and crustaceans and tadpoles, and all kinds of insects could be planted. But nothing else.

The *Ludred* swam away through emptiness.

There should have been another planting centuries later. There should have been a ship from the Zoölogical Branch of the Ecological Service. It should have landed birds and beasts and reptiles. It should have added pelagic mammals to the seas. There should have been herbivorous animals to live on the grasses and plants which would have thriven, and carnivorous animals to live on them in turn. There should have been a careful stocking of the planet with animal life, and repeated visits at intervals of a century or so to make sure that a true ecological balance had been established. And then when the balance was fixed men would come and destroy it for their own benefit.

But there was an accident.

Ships had improved again. Even small private spacecraft now journeyed tens of light-years on holiday journeys. Personal cruisers traveled hundreds. Liners ran matter-of-factly on ship-lines tens of thousands of light-years long. An exploring-ship was on its way to a second island universe. (It did not come back.) The inhabited planets were all members of a tenuous organization which limited itself to affairs of space, without attempting to interfere in surface matters. That tenuous organization moved the Ecological Preparation Service files to Algol IV as a matter of convenience. In the moving, a card-file was upset. The cards it contained were picked up and replaced, but one was missed. It was not picked up. It was left behind.

So the planet which had no name was forgotten. No other ship came to prepare it for ultimate human occupancy. It circled its sun, unheeded and unthought-of. Cloudbanks covered it from pole to pole. There were hazy markings in some places, where high plateaus penetrated its clouds. But that was all. From space the planet was essentially featureless. Seen from afar it was merely a round white ball—white from its cloudbanks—and nothing else.

But on its surface, on its lowlands, it was pure nightmare. But this fact did not matter for a very long time.

Ultimately, it mattered a great deal—to the crew of the space-liner *Icarus*. The *Icarus* was a splendid ship of its time. It bore passengers headed for one of the Galaxy's spiral arms, and it cut across the normal lanes and headed through charted but unvisited parts of the Galaxy toward its destination. And it had one of the very, very, very few accidents known to happen to space-craft licensed for travel off the normal space-lanes. It suffered shipwreck in space, and its passengers and crew were forced to take to the lifecraft.

The lifeboats' range was limited. They landed on the planet that the *Tethys* had first examined, that the *Orana* and the *Ludred* had seeded, and of which there was no longer any record in the card-files of the Ecological Service. Their fuel was exhausted. They could not leave. They could not signal for help. They had to stay there. And the planet was a place of nightmares.

After a time the few people—some few thousands— who knew that there was a space-liner named *Icarus*, gave it up for lost. They forgot about it. Everybody forgot. Even the passengers and crew of the ship forgot it. Not immediately, of course. For the first few generations their descendants cherished hopes of rescue. But the planet which had no name—the forgotten planet—did not encourage the cherishing of hope.

After forty-odd generations, nobody remembered the *Icarus* anywhere. The wreckage of the lifeboats was long since hidden under the seething, furiously striving fungi of the soil. The human beings had forgotten not only their ancestors' ship, but very nearly everything their ancestors had brought to this world: the use of metals, the existence of fire, and even the fact that there was such a thing as sunshine. They lived in the lowlands, deep under the cloudbank, amid surroundings which were riotous, swarming, frenzied horror. They had become savages.

They were less than savages, because they had forgotten their destiny as men.

I N ALL HIS lifetime of perhaps twenty years, it had never occurred to Burl to wonder what his grandfather had thought about his surroundings. The grandfather had come to an untimely end in a fashion which Burl remembered as a succession of screams coming more and more faintly to his ears, while he was being carried away at the topmost speed of which his mother was capable.

Burl had rarely or never thought of his grandfather since. Surely he had never wondered what his great-grandfather had thought, and most surely of all he never speculated upon what his many-times-removed great-grandfather had thought when his lifeboat landed from the *Icarus*. Burl had never heard of the *Icarus*. He had done very little thinking of any sort. When he did think, it was mostly agonized effort to contrive a way to escape some immediate and paralyzing danger. When horror did not press upon him, it was better not to think, because there wasn't much but horror to think about.

9

At the moment, he was treading cautiously over a brownish carpet of fungus, creeping furtively toward the stream which he knew only by the generic name of "water." It was the only water he knew. Towering far above his head, three man-heights high, great toadstools hid the gray sky from his sight. Clinging to the yard-thick stalks of the toadstools were still other fungi, parasites upon the growths that once had been parasites themselves.

Burl appeared a fairly representative specimen of the descendants of the long-forgotten *Icarus* crew. He wore a single garment twisted about his middle, made from the wing-fabric of a great moth which the members of his tribe had slain as it emerged from its cocoon. His skin was fair, without a trace of sunburn. In all his lifetime he had never seen the sun, though he surely had seen the sky often enough. It was rarely hidden from him save by giant fungi, like those about him now, and sometimes by the gigantic cabbages which were nearly the only green growths he knew. To him a normal landscape contained only fantastic pallid mosses, and misshapen fungus growths, and colossal moulds and yeasts.

He moved onward. Despite his caution, his shoulder once touched a cream-colored toadstool stalk, giving the whole fungus a tiny shock. Instantly a fine and impalpable powder fell upon him from the umbrellalike top above. It was the season when the toadstools sent out their spores. He paused to brush them from his head and shoulders. They were, of course, deadly poison.

Burl knew such matters with an immediate and specific and detailed certainty. He knew practically nothing else. He was ignorant of the use of fire, of metals, and even of the uses of stone and wood. His language was a scanty group of a few hundred labial sounds, conveying no abstractions and few concrete ideas. He knew nothing of wood, because there was no wood in the territory furtively inhabited by his tribe. This was the lowlands. Trees did not thrive here. Not even grasses and tree-ferns could compete with mushrooms and toadstools and their kin. Here was a soil of rusts and yeasts. Here were toadstool forests and fungus jungles. They grew with feverish intensity beneath a cloud-hidden sky, while above them fluttered butterflies no less enlarged than they, moths as much magnified, and other creatures which could thrive on their corruption.

The only creatures on the planet which crawled or ran or flew—save only Burl's fugitive kind—were insects. They had been here before men came, and they had adapted to the planet's extraordinary ways. With a world made ready before their first progenitors arrived, insects had thriven incredibly. With unlimited food supplies, they had grown large. With increased size had come increased opportunity for survival, and enlargement became hereditary. Other than fungoid growths, the solitary vegetables were the sports of unstable varieties of the plants left behind by the *Ludred*. There were enormous cabbages, with leaves the size of ship-sails, on which stolid grubs and caterpillars ate themselves to maturity, and then swung below in strong cocoons to sleep the sleep of metamorphosis. The tiniest butterflies of Earth had increased their size here until their wings spread feet across, and some—like the emperor moths—stretched out purple wings which were yards in span. Burl himself would have been dwarfed beneath a great moth's wing.

But he wore a gaudy fabric made of one. The moths

and giant butterflies were harmless to men. Burl's fellow tribesmen sometimes came upon a cocoon when it was just about to open, and if they dared they waited timorously beside it until the creature inside broke through its sleeping-shell and came out into the light.

Then, before it gathered energy from the air and before its wings swelled to strength and firmness, the tribesmen fell upon it. They tore the delicate wings from its body and the still-flaccid limbs from their places. And when it lay helpless before them they fled away to feast on its juicy, meat-filled limbs.

They dared not linger, of course. They left their prey helpless—staring strangely at the world about it through its many-faceted eyes—before the scavengers came to contest its ownership. If nothing more deadly appeared, surely the ants would come. Some of them were only inches long, but others were the size of fox-terriers. All of them had to be avoided by men. They would carry the moth-carcass away to their underground cities, triumphantly, in shreds and morsels.

But most of the insect world was neither so helpless nor so unthreatening. Burl knew of wasps almost the length of his own body, with stings that were instantly fatal. To every species of wasp, however, some other insect is predestined prey. Wasps need not be dreaded too much. And bees were similarly aloof. They were hard put to it for existence, those bees. Since few flowers bloomed, they were reduced to expedients that once were considered signs of degeneracy in their race: bubbling yeasts and fouler things, or occasionally the nectarless blooms of the rank giant cabbages. Burl knew the bees. They droned overhead, nearly as large as he was, their bulging eyes gazing at him and everything else in abstracted preoccupation.

There were crickets, and beetles, and spiders. . . . Burl knew spiders! His grandfather had been the prey of a hunting tarantula which had leaped with incredible ferocity from its tunnel in the ground. A vertical pit, a yard in diameter, went down for twenty feet. At the bottom of the lair the monster waited for the tiny sounds that would warn him of prey approaching his hiding-place.

Burl's grandfather had been careless. The terrible shrieks he uttered as he was seized still lingered vaguely in Burl's mind. And he had seen, too, the webs of another species of spider—inch-thick cables of dirty silk—and watched from a safe distance as the misshapen monster sucked the juices from a three-foot cricket its trap had caught. He remembered the stripes of yellow and black and silver that crossed upon its abdomen. He had been fascinated and horrified by the blind struggling of the cricket, tangled in hopeless coils of gummy cord, before the spider began its feast.

Burl knew these dangers. They were part of his life. It was this knowledge that made life possible. He knew the ways to evade these dangers. But if he yielded to carelessness for one moment, or if he relaxed his caution for one instant, he would be one with his ancestors. They were the long-forgotten meals of inhuman monsters.

Now, to be sure, Burl moved upon an errand that probably no other of his tribe would have imagined. The day before, he had crouched behind a shapeless mound of intertangled growths and watched a duel between two huge horned beetles. Their bodies were feet long. Their carapaces were waist-high to Burl when they crawled. Their mandibles, gaping laterally, clicked and clashed upon each other's impenetrable armor. Their legs crashed like so many cymbals as they struck against each other. They fought over some particularly attractive bit of carrion.

Burl had watched with wide eyes until a gaping hole appeared in the armor of the smaller one. It uttered a grating outcry—or seemed to. The noise was actually the tearing of its shell between the mandibles of the victor.

The wounded creature struggled more and more feebly. When it ceased to offer battle, the conqueror placidly began to dine before its prey had ceased to live. But this was the custom of creatures on this planet.

Burl watched, timorous but hopeful. When the meal was finished, he darted in quickly as the diner lumbered away. He was almost too late, even then. An ant—the forerunner of many—already inspected the fragments with excitedly vibrating antennae.

Burl needed to move quickly and he did. Ants were stupid and short-sighted insects; few of them were hunters. Save when offered battle, most of them were scavengers only. They hunted the scenes of nightmare for the dead and dying only, but fought viciously if their prey were questioned. And always there were others on the way.

Some were arriving now. Hearing the tiny clickings of their approach, Burl was hasty. Over-hasty. He seized a loosened fragment and fled. It was merely the horn, the snout of the dead and eaten creature. But it was loose and easily carried. He ran.

Later he inspected his find with disappointment. There was little meat clinging to it. It was merely the horn of a Minotaur beetle, shaped like the horn of a rhinoceros.

Plucking out the shreds left by its murderer, he pricked his hand. Pettishly, he flung it aside. The time of darkness was near, so he crept to the hiding place of his tribe to huddle with them until light came again.

There were only twenty of them; four or five men and six or seven women. The rest were girls or children. Burl had been wondering at the strange feelings that came over him when he looked at one of the girls. She was younger than Burl—perhaps eighteen—and fleeter of foot. They talked together sometimes and, once or twice, Burl shared an especially succulent find of foodstuffs with her.

He could share nothing with her now. She stared at him in the deepening night when he crept to the labyrinthine hiding place the tribe now used in a mushroom forest. He considered that she looked hungry and hoped that he would have food to share. And he was bitterly ashamed that he could offer nothing. He held himself a little apart from the rest, because of his shame. Since he too was hungry, it was some time before he slept. Then he dreamed.

Next morning he found the horn where he had thrown it disgustedly the day before. It was sticking in the flabby trunk of a toadstool. He pulled it out. In his dream he had used it. . . .

Presently he tried to use it. Sometimes—not often—the men of the tribe used the saw-toothed edge of a cricket-leg, or the leg of a grasshopper, to sever tough portions of an edible mushroom. The horn had no cutting edge, but Burl had used it in his dream. He was not quite capable of distinguishing clearly between reality and dreams; so he tried to duplicate what happened in the dream. Remembering that it had stuck into the mushroom-stalk, he thrust it. It stabbed. He remembered distinctly how the larger beetle had used its horn as a weapon. It had stabbed, too.

He considered absorbedly. He could not imagine himself fighting one of the dangerous insects, of course. Men did not fight, on the forgotten planet. They ran away. They hid. But somehow Burl formed a fantastic picture of himself stabbing food with this horn, as he had stabbed a mushroom. It was longer than his arm and though naturally clumsy in his hand, it would have been a deadly weapon in the grip of a man prepared to do battle.

Battle did not occur to Burl. But the idea of stabbing food with it was clear. There could be food that would not fight back. Presently he had an inspiration. His face brightened. He began to make his way toward the tiny river that ran across the plain in which the tribe of humans lived by foraging in competition with the ants. Yellow-bellied newts—big enough to be lusted for—swam in its waters. The swimming larvae of a thousand kinds of creatures floated on the sluggish surface or crawled over the bottom.

There were deadly things there, too. Giant crayfish snapped their claws at the unwary. One of them could sever Burl's arm with ease. Mosquitoes sometimes hummed high above the water. Mosquitoes had a four-inch wingspread, now, though they were dying out for lack of plant-juices on which the males of their species fed. But they were formidable. Burl had learned to crush them between fragments of fungus.

He crept slowly through the forest of toadstools. What should have been grass underfoot was brownish rust. Orange and red and purple moulds clustered about the bases of the creamy mushroom-trunks. Once, Burl paused to run his weapon through a fleshy column and reassure himself that what he planned was possible.

He made his way furtively through the bulbous growths. Once he heard clickings and froze to stillness. Four or five ants, minims only eight inches long, were returning by an habitual pathway to their city. They moved sturdily along, heavily laden, over the route marked by the scent of formic acid left by their fellow-townsmen. Burl waited until they had passed, then went on.

He came to the bank of the river. It flowed slowly, green scum covering a great deal of its surface in the backwaters, occasionally broken by a slowly enlarging bubble released from decomposing matter on the bottom. In the center of the stream the current ran a little more swiftly and the water itself seemed clear. Over it ran many water-spiders. They had not shared in the general increase of size in the insect world. Depending as they did on the surface tension of the water for support, to have grown larger and heavier would have destroyed them.

Burl surveyed the scene. His search was four parts for danger and only one part for a way to test his brilliant notion, but that was natural. Where he stood, the green scum covered the stream for many yards. Down-river a little, though, the current came close to the bank. Here he could not see whatever swam or crawled or wriggled underwater; there he might.

There was an outcropping rock forming a support for crawling stuff, which in turn supported shelf-fungi making wide steps almost down to the water's edge. Burl was making his way cautiously toward them when he saw one of the edible mushrooms which formed so large a part of his diet.

He paused to break off a flabby white piece large enough to feed him for many days. It was the custom of his people, when they found a store of food, to hide with it and not venture out again to danger until it was all eaten. Burl was tempted to do just that with his booty. He could give Saya of this food and they would eat together. They might hide together until it was all consumed.

But there was a swirling in the water under the descending platforms of shelf-fungi. A very remarkable sensation came to Burl. He may have been the only man in many generations to be aware of the high ambition to stab something to eat. He may have been a throw-back to ancestors who had known bravery, which had no survival-value here. But Burl had imagined carrying Saya food which he had stabbed with the spear of a Minotaur beetle. It was an extraordinary idea.

It was new, too. Not too long ago, when he was younger, Burl would have thought of the tribe instead. He'd have thought of old Jon, bald-headed and wheezing and timorous, and how that patriarch would pat his arm exuberantly when handed food; or old Tama, wrinkled and querulous, whose look of settled dissatisfaction would vanish at sight of a tidbit; of Dik and Tet, the tribe-members next younger, who would squabble zestfully over the fragments allotted them.

But now he imagined Saya looking astonished and glad when he grandly handed her more food than she could possibly eat. She would admire him enormously!

Of course he did not imagine himself fighting to get food for Saya. He meant only to stab something edible in the water. Things in the water did not fight things on land.

Since he would not be in the water, he would not be in a fight. It was a completely delectable idea, which no man within memory had ever entertained before. If Burl accomplished it, his tribe would admire him. Saya would admire him. Everybody, observing that he had found a new source of food, would even envy him until he showed them how to do it too. Burl's fellow-humans were preoccupied with the filling of their stomachs. The preservation of their lives came second. The perpetuation of the race came a bad third in their consideration. They were herded together in a leaderless group, coming to the same hiding-place nightly only that they might share the finds of the lucky and gather comfort from their numbers. They had no weapons. Even Burl did not consider his spear a weapon. It was a tool for stabbing something to eat only. Yet he did not think of it in that way exactly. His tribe did not even consciously use tools. Sometimes they used stones to crack open the limbs of great insects they found incompletely devoured. They did not even carry rocks about with them for that purpose. Only Burl had a vague idea of taking something to some place to do something with it. It was unprecedented. Burl was at least an atavar. He may have been a genius.

But he was not a high-grade genius. Certainly not yet.

He reached a spot from which he could look down into the water. He looked behind and all about, listening, then lay down to stare into the shallow depths. Once a huge crayfish, a good eight feet long, moved leisurely across his vision. Small fishes and even the huge newts fled before it.

After a long time the normal course of underwater life resumed. The wriggling caddis-flies in their quaintly ambi-

tious houses reappeared. Little flecks of silver swam into
view—a school of tiny fish. Then a larger fish appeared,
moving slowly in the stream.

Burl's eyes glistened; his mouth watered. He reached
down with his long weapon. It barely broke through the still
surface of the water below. Disappointment filled him, yet
the nearness and apparent probability of success spurred
him on.

He examined the shelf-fungi beneath him. Rising, he
moved to a point above them and tested one with his spear.
It resisted. Burl felt about tentatively with his foot, then
dared to put his whole weight on the topmost. It held
firmly. He clambered down upon the lower ones, then lay
flat and peered over the edge.

The large fish, fully as long as Burl's arm, swam slowly
to and fro beneath him. Burl had seen the former owner of
this spear strive to thrust it into his adversary. The beetle
had been killed by the more successful stab of a similar
weapon. Burl had tried this upon toadstools, practising with
it. When the silver fish drifted close by again, he thrust
sharply downward.

The spear seemed to bend when it entered the water. It
missed its mark by inches, much to Burl's astonishment. He
tried again. Once more the spear seemed diverted by the
water. He grew angry with the fish for eluding his efforts to
kill it.

This anger was as much the reaction of a throw-back to
a less fearful time as the idea of killing itself. But Burl
scowled at the fish. Repeated strokes had left it untouched.
It was unwary. It did not even swim away.

Then it came to rest directly beneath his hand. He
thrust directly downward, with all his strength. This time

the spear, entering vertically, did not appear to bend, but went straight down. Its point penetrated the scales of the swimming fish, transfixing the creature completely.

An uproar began with the fish wriggling desperately as Burl tried to draw it up to his perch. In his excitement he did not notice a tiny ripple a little distance away. The monster crayfish, attracted by the disturbance, was coming back.

The unequal combat continued. Burl hung on desperately to the end of his spear. Then there was a tremor in the shelf-fungus on which he lay. It yielded, collapsed, and fell into the stream with a mighty splash. Burl went under, his eyes wide open, facing death. As he sank he saw the gaping, horrible claws of the crustacean, huge enough to sever any of Burl's limbs with a single snap.

He opened his mouth to scream, but no sound came out. Only bubbles floated up to the surface. He beat the unresisting fluid in a frenzy of horror with his hands and feet as the colossal crayfish leisurely approached.

His arms struck a solid object. He clutched it convulsively. A second later he had swung it between himself and the crustacean. He felt the shock as the claws closed upon the cork-like fungus. Then he felt himself drawn upward as the crayfish disgustedly released its hold and the shelf-fungus floated slowly upward. Having given way beneath him, it had been pushed below when he fell, only to rise within his reach just when most needed.

Burl's head popped above-water and he saw a larger bit of the fungus floating nearby. Even less securely anchored to the river-bank then the shelf to which he had trusted himself, it had broken away when he fell. It was larger and floated higher.

He seized it, crazily trying to climb up. It tilted under

his weight and very nearly overturned. He paid no heed. With desperate haste he clawed and kicked until he could draw himself clear of the water.

As he pulled himself up on the furry, orange-brown surface, a sharp blow struck his foot. The crayfish, disappointed at finding nothing tasty in the shelf-fungus, had made a languid stroke at Burl's foot wriggling in the water. Failing to grasp the fleshy member, it went annoyedly away.

Burl floated downstream, perched weaponless and alone upon a flimsy raft of degenerate fungus; floated slowly down a stagnant river in which death swam, between banks of sheer peril, past long reaches above which death floated on golden wings.

It was a long while before he recovered his self-possession. Then—and this was an action individual in Burl: none of his tribesmen would have thought of it—he looked for his spear.

It was floating in the water, still transfixing the fish whose capture had brought him to this present predicament. That silvery shape, so violent before, now floated belly-up, all life gone.

Burl's mouth watered as he gazed at the fish. He kept it in view constantly while the unsteady craft spun slowly downstream in the current. Lying flat he tried to reach out and grasp the end of the spear when it circled toward him.

The raft tilted, nearly capsizing. A little later he discovered that it sank more readily on one side than the other. This was due, of course, to the greater thickness of one side. The part next to the river-bank had been thicker and was, therefore, more buoyant.

He lay with his head above that side of the raft. It did

not sink into the water. Wriggling as far to the edge as he dared, he reached out and out. He waited impatiently for the slower rotation of his float to coincide with the faster motion of the speared fish. The spear-end came closer, and closer. . . . He reached out—and the raft dipped dangerously. But his fingers touched the spear-end. He got a precarious hold, pulled it toward him.

Seconds later he was tearing strips of scaly flesh from the side of the fish and cramming the greasy stuff into his mouth with vast enjoyment. He had lost the edible mushroom. It floated several yards away. He ate contentedly nonetheless.

He thought of the tribesfolk as he ate. This was more than he could finish alone. Old Tama would coax him avidly for more than her share. She had few teeth left. She would remind him anxiously of her gifts of food to him when he was younger. Dik and Tet—being boys—would clamorously demand of him where he'd gotten it. How? He would give some to Cori, who had younger children, and she would give them most of the gift. And Saya—.

Burl gloated especially over Saya's certain reaction.

Then he realized that with every second he was being carried farther away from her. The nearer river-bank moved past him. He could tell by the motion of the vividly colored growths upon the shore.

Overhead, the sun were merely a brighter patch in the haze-filled sky. In the pinkish light all about, Burl looked for the familiar and did not find it, and dolefully knew that he was remote from Saya and going farther all the time.

There were a multitude of flying objects to be seen in the miasmatic air. In the daytime a thin mist always hung above the lowlands. Burl had never seen any object as much as three miles distant. The air was never clear enough to permit it. But there was much to be seen even within the limiting mist.

Now and then a cricket or a grasshopper made its bulletlike flight from one spot to another. Huge butterflies fluttered gaily above the silent, loathsome ground. Bees lumbered anxiously about, seeking the cross-shaped flowers of the giant cabbages which grew so rarely. Occasionally a slender-waisted, yellow-bellied wasp flashed swiftly by.

But Burl did not heed any of them. Sitting dismally upon his fungus raft, floating in midstream, an incongruous figure of pink skin and luridly-tinted loincloth, with a greasy dead fish beside him, he was filled with a panicky anguish because the river carried him away from the one girl of his tiny tribe whose glances roused a commotion in his breast.

The day wore on. Once, he saw a band of large red amazon ants moving briskly over a carpet of blue-green mould to raid the city of a species of black ants. The eggs they would carry away from the city would hatch and the small black creatures would become the slaves of the brigands who had stolen them.

Later, strangely-shaped, swollen branches drifted slowly into view. They were outlined sharply against the steaming mist behind them. He knew what they were: a hard-rinded fungus growing upon itself in peculiar mockery of the trees which Burl had never seen because no trees could survive the conditions of the lowland.

Much later, as the day drew to an end, Burl ate again of the oily fish. The taste was pleasant compared to the insipid mushrooms he usually ate. Even though he stuffed himself,

the fish was so large that the greater part remained still uneaten.

The spear was beside him. Although it had brought him
trouble, he still associated it with the food it had secured
rather than the difficulty into which it had led him. When
he had eaten his fill, he picked it up to examine again. The
oil-covered point remained as sharp as before.

Not daring to use it again from so unsteady a raft, he set
it aside as he stripped a sinew from his loincloth to hang the
fish around his neck. The would leave his arms free. Then
he sat cross-legged, fumbling with the spear as he watched
the shores go past.

A Man Escapes

2

I T WAS NEAR to sunset. Burl had never seen the sun, so it did not occur to him to think of the coming of night as the setting of anything. To him it was the letting down of darkness from the sky.

The process was invariable. Overhead there was always a thick and unbroken bank of vapor which seemed featureless until sunset. Then, toward the west, the brightness overhead turned orange and then pink, while to the east it simply faded to a deeper gray. As nightfall progressed, the red colorings grew deeper, moving toward mid-sky. Ultimately, scattered blotches of darkness began to spot that reddening sky as it grew darker in tone, going down toward that impossible redness which is indistinguishable from black. It was slowly achieving that redness.

Today Burl watched as never before. On the oily surface of the river the colors and shadings of dusk were reflected with incredible faithfulness. The round tops of toadstools along the shore glowed pink. Dragonflies glinted in swift

27

and angular flight, the metallic sheen of their bodies flashing in the redness. Great, yellow butterflies sailed lightly above the stream. In every direction upon the water appeared the scrap-formed boats of a thousand caddis-flies, floating at the surface while they might. Burl could have thrust his hand down into their cavities to seize the white worms nesting there.

The bulk of a tardy bee droned heavily overhead. He saw the long proboscis and the hairy hind-legs with their scanty load of pollen. The great, multi-faceted eyes held an expression of stupid preoccupation.

The crimson radiance grew dim and the color overhead faded toward black. Now the stalks of ten thousand domed mushrooms lined the river-bank. Beneath them spread fungi of all colors, from the rawest red to palest blue, now all fading slowly to a monochromatic background as the darkness deepened.

The buzzing and fluttering and flapping of the insects of the day died down. From a million hiding places there crept out—into the night—the soft and furry bodies of great moths who preened themselves and smoothed their feathery antennae before taking to the air. The strong-limbed crickets set up their thunderous noise, grown gravely bass with the increasing size of the noise-making organs. Then there began to gather on the water those slender spirals of deeper mist which would presently blanket the stream in fog.

Night arrived. The clouds above grew wholly black. Gradually, the languid fall of large, warm raindrops—they would fall all through the night—began. The edge of the stream became a place where disks of cold blue flame appeared.

The mushrooms on the river bank were faintly phosphorescent, shedding a ghostly light over the ground below them. Here and there, lambent chilly flames appeared in mid-air, drifting idly above the festering earth. On other planets men call them "Will-o'-the-wisps," but on this planet mankind had no name for them at all.

Then huge, pulsating glows appeared in the blackness: fireflies that Burl knew to be as long as his spear. They glided slowly through the darkness over the stream, shedding intermittent light over Burl crouched on his drifting raft. On the shore, too, tiny paired lights glowed eagerly upward as the wingless females of the species crawled to where their signals could be seen. And there were other glowing things. Fox-fire burned in the night, consuming nothing. Even the water of the river glowed with marine organisms—adapted to fresh water here—contributing their mites of brilliance.

The air was full of flying creatures. The beat of invisible wings came through the night. Above, about, on every side the swarming, feverish life of the insect world went on ceaselessly, while Burl rocked back and forth upon his unstable raft, wanting to weep because he was being carried farther away from Saya whom he could picture looking for him, now, among the hidden, furtive members of the tribe. About him sounded the discordant, machine-like mating cries of creatures trying to serve life in the midst of death and the horrible noises of those who met death and were devoured in the dark.

Burl was accustomed to such tumult. But he was not accustomed to such despair as he felt at being lost from Saya of the swift feet and white teeth and shy smile. He lay disconsolate on his bobbing craft for the greater part of the night. It was long past midnight when the raft struck gently, swung, and then remained grounded upon a shallow in the stream.

When light came back in the morning, Burl gazed about him fearfully. He was some twenty yards from the shore and thick greenish scum surrounded his disintegrating vessel. The river had widened greatly until the opposite bank was hidden in the morning mist, but the nearer shore seemed firm and no more full of dangers than the territory inhabited by Burl's tribe.

He tested the depth of the water with his spear, struck by the multiple usefulness of the weapon. The water was no more than ankle-deep.

Shivering a little, Burl stepped down into the green scum and made for the shore at top speed. He felt something soft clinging to his bare foot. With a frantic rush he ran even faster and stumbled upon the shore with horror not at his heels but on one. He stared down at his foot. A shapeless, flesh-colored pad clung to the skin. As he watched, it swelled visibly, the pink folds becoming a deeper shade.

It was no more than a leech, the size of his palm, sharing in the enlargement nearly all the insect and fungoid world had undergone, but Burl did not know that. He thrust at it with the edge of his spear, scraping it frantically away. As it fell off Burl stared in horror first at the blotch of blood on his foot, then at the thing writhing and pulsating on the ground. He fled.

A short while later he stumbled into one of the familiar toadstool forests and paused, uncertainly. The towering toadstools were not strange to Burl. He fell to eating. The sight of food always produced hunger in him—a provision of nature to make up for the lack of any instinct to store food away. In human beings the storage of food has to be dictated by intellect. The lower orders of creatures are not required to think.

Even eating, though, Burl's heart was small within him. He was far from his tribe and Saya. By the measurements of his remotest ancestors, no more than forty miles separated them. But Burl did not think in such terms. He'd never had occasion to do so. He'd come down the river to a far land filled with unknown dangers. And he was alone.

All about him was food, an excellent reason for gladness. But being solitary was reason enough for distress. Although Burl was a creature to whom reflection was normally of no especial value and, therefore, not practised in thought, this was a situation providing an emotional paradox. A good fourth of the mushrooms in this particular forest were edible. Burl should have gloated over this vast stock of food. But he was isolated, alone; in particular, he was far away from Saya, therefore, he should have wept. But he could not gloat because he was away from Saya and he could not mourn because he was surrounded by food.

He was subject to a stimulus to which apparently only humankind can respond: an emotional dilemma. Other creatures can respond to objective situations where there is the need to choose a course of action: flight or fighting, hiding or pursuit. But only man can be disturbed by not knowing which of two emotions to feel. Burl had reason to feel two entirely different emotional states at the same time. He had to resolve the paradox. The problem was inside him, not out. So he thought.

He would bring Saya here! He would bring her and the tribe to this place where there was food in vast quantity!

Instantly pictures flooded into his mind. He could actually see old Jon, his bald head naked as a mushroom itself, stuffing his belly with the food which was so plentiful here. He imagined Cori feeding her children. Tama's complaints stilled by mouthfuls of food. Tet and Dik, stuffed to repletion, throwing scraps of foodstuff at each other. He pictured the tribe zestfully feasting—and Saya would be very glad.

It was remarkable that Burl was able to think of his feelings instead of his sensations. His tribesmen were closer to it than equally primitive folk had been back on Earth, but they did not often engage in thought. Their waking lives were filled with nerve-racked physical responses to physical phenomena. They were hungry and they saw or smelled food: they were alive and they perceived the presence of death. In the one case they moved toward the sensory stimulus of food; in the other they fled from the detected stimulus of danger. They responded immediately to the world about them. Burl, for the first significant time in his life, had responded to inner feelings. He had resolved conflicting emotions by devising a purpose that would end their conflict. He determined to do something because he wanted to and not because he had to.

It was the most important event upon the planet in generations.

With the directness of a child, or a savage, Burl moved to carry out his purpose. The fish still slung about his neck scraped against his chest. Fingering it tentatively, he got himself thoroughly greasy in the process, but could not eat. Although he was not hungry now, perhaps Saya was. He could give it to her. He imagined her eager delight, the image reinforcing his resolve. He had come to this far place down the river flowing sluggishly past this riotously colored bank. To return to the tribe he would go back up that bank, staying close to the stream.

He was remarkably exultant as he forced a way through the awkward aisles of the mushroom-forest, but his eyes and ears were still open for any possible danger. Several times he heard the omnipresent clicking of ants scavenging in the mushroom-glades, but they could be ignored. At best they were short-sighted. If he dropped his fish, they would become absorbed in it. There was only one kind of ant he needed to fear—the army ant, which sometimes traveled in hordes of millions, eating everything in their path.

But there was nothing of the sort here. The mushroom forest came to an end. A cheerful grasshopper munched delicately at some dainty it had found—the barrel-sized young shoot of a cabbage-plant. Its hind legs were bunched beneath it in perpetual readiness for flight. A monster wasp appeared a hundred feet overhead, checked in its flight, and plunged upon the luckless banqueter.

There was a struggle, but it was brief. The grasshopper strained terribly in the grip of the wasp's six barbed legs. The wasp's flexible abdomen curved delicately. Its sting entered the jointed armor of its prey just beneath the head with all the deliberate precision of a surgeon's scalpel. A ganglion lay there; the wasp-poison entered it. The grasshopper went limp. It was not dead, of course, simply paralyzed. Permanently paralyzed. The wasp preened itself, then matter-of-factly grasped its victim and flew away. The grasshopper would be incubator and food-supply for an egg to be laid. Presently, in a huge mud castle, a small white worm would feed upon the living, motionless victim of its mother—who would never see it, or care, or remember. . . .

Burl went on.

The ground grew rougher; progress became painful. He clambered arduously up steep slopes—all of forty or fifty feet high—and made his way cautiously down to the farther sides. Once he climbed through a tangled mass of mushrooms so closely placed and so small that he had to break them apart with blows of his spear in order to pass. As they crumbled, torrents of a fiery-red liquid showered down upon him, rolling off his greasy breast and sinking into the ground.

A strange self-confidence now took possession of Burl. He walked less cautiously and more boldly. He had thought and he had struck something, feeling the vainglorious self-satisfaction of a child. He pictured himself leading his tribe to this place of very much food—he had no real idea of the distance—and he strutted all alone amid the nightmare-growths of the planet that had been forgotten.

Presently he could see the river. He had climbed to the top of a red-clay mound perhaps a hundred feet high. One side was crumbled where the river overflowed. At some past flood-time the water had lapped at the base of the cliff along which Burl was strutting. But now there was a quarter-mile of space between himself and the water. And there was something else in mid-air.

The cliffside was thickly coated with fungi in a riotous confusion of white and yellow and orange and green. From a point halfway up the cliff the inch-thick cable of a spider-web stretched down to anchorage on the ground below.

There were other cables beyond this one and circling about their radial pattern the snare-cords of the web formed a perfect logarithmic spiral.

Somewhere among the fungi of the cliffside the huge spider who had built this web awaited the entrapment of prey. When some unfortunate creature struggled frenziedly in its snare it would emerge. Until then it waited in a motionless, implacable patience; utterly certain of victims, utterly merciless to them.

Burl strutted on the edge of the cliff, a rather foolish pink-skinned creature with an oily fish slung about his neck and the draggled fragment of moth's wing draping his middle. He waved the long shard of beetle armor exultantly above his head.

The activity was not very sensible. It served no purpose. But if Burl was a genius among his fellows, then he still had a great deal to learn before his genius would be effective. Now he looked down scornfully upon the shining white trap below. He had struck a fish, killing it. When he hit mushrooms they fell into pieces before him. Nothing could frighten him! He would go to Saya and bring her to this land where food grew in abundance.

Sixty paces away from Burl, near the edge of the cliff, a shaft sank vertically into the soil of the clay-mound. It was carefully rounded and lined with silk. Thirty feet down, it enlarged itself into a chamber where the engineer and proprietor of the shaft might rest. The top of the hole was closed by a trap-door, stained with mud and earth to imitate the surrounding soil. A sharp eye would have been needed to detect the opening. But a keener eye now peered out from the crack at its edge.

That eye belonged to the proprietor.

Eight hairy legs surrounded the body of the monster hanging motionless at the top of the silk-lined shaft. Its belly was a huge misshapen globe colored a dirty brown. Two pairs of mandibles stretched before its mouth-parts; two eyes glittered in the semi-darkness of the burrow. Over the whole body spread a rough and mangy fur.

It was a thing of implacable malignance, of incredible ferocity. It was the brown hunting spider, the American tarantula, enlarged here upon the forgotten planet so that its body was two feet and more in diameter. Its legs, outstretched, would cover a circle three yards across. The glittering eyes followed as Burl strutted forward on the edge of the cliff, puffed up with a sense of his own importance.

Spread out below, the white snare of the spinning-spider impressed Burl as amusing. He knew the spider wouldn't leave its web to attack him. Reaching down, he broke off a bit of fungus growing at his feet. Where he broke it away oozed a soupy liquid full of tiny maggots in a delirium of feasting. Burl flung it down into the web, laughing as the black bulk of the watchful spider swung down from its hiding place to investigate.

The tarantula, peering from its burrow, quivered with impatience. Burl drew nearer, gleefully using his spear as a lever to pry off bits of trash to fall down the cliffside into the giant web. The spider below moved leisurely from one spot to another, investigating each new missile with its palpi and then ignoring it as lifeless and undesirable prey.

Burl leaped and laughed aloud as a particularly large lump of putrid fungus narrowly missed the black-and-silver shape below. Then—

The trapdoor fell into place with a faint sound. Burl

whirled about, his laughter transformed instantly into a scream. Moving toward him furiously, its eight legs scrambling, was the monster tarantula. Its mandibles gaped wide; the poison fangs were unsheathed. It was thirty paces away—twenty paces—ten.

Eyes glittering, it leaped, all eight legs extended to seize the prey.

Burl screamed again and thrust out his arms to ward off the creature. It was pure blind horror. There was no genius in that gesture! Because of sheer terror his grip upon the spear had become agonized. The spear-point shot out and the tarantula fell upon it. Nearly a quarter of the spear entered the body of the ferocious thing.

Stuck upon the spear the spider writhed horribly, still striving to reach the paralytically frozen Burl. The great mandibles clashed. Furious bubbling noises came from it. The hairy legs clutched at his arm. He cried out hoarsely in ultimate fear and staggered backward—and the edge of the cliff gave way beneath him.

He hurtled downward, still clutching the spear, incapable of letting go. Even while falling the writhing thing still struggled maniacally to reach him. Down through emptiness they fell together, Burl glassy-eyed with panic. Then there was a strangely elastic crash and crackling. They had fallen into the web at which Burl had been laughing so scornfully only a little while before.

Burl couldn't think. He only struggled insanely in the gummy coils of the web. But the snare-cords were spiral threads, enormously elastic, exuding impossibly sticky stuff, like bird-lime, from between twisted constituent fibres. Near him—not two yards away—the creature he had wounded thrashed and fought to reach him, even while shuddering in anguish.

Burl had reached the absolute limit of panic. His arms and breast were greasy from the oily fish; the sticky web did not adhere to them. But his legs and body were inextricably tangled by his own frantic struggling in the gummy and adhesive elastic threads. They had been spread for prey. He was prey.

He paused in his blind struggle, gasping from pure exhaustion. Then he saw, not five yards away, the silvery-and-black monster he had mocked so recently now patiently waiting for him to cease his struggles. The tarantula and the man were one to its eyes—one struggling thing that had fallen opportunely into its trap. They were moving but feebly, now. The web-spider advanced delicately, swinging its huge bulk nimbly, paying out a silken cable behind it as it approached.

Burl's arms were free; he waved them wildly, shrieking at the monster. The spider paused. Burl's moving arms suggested mandibles that might wound.

Spiders take few chances. This one drew near cautiously, then stopped. Its spinnerets became busy and with one of its eight legs, used like an arm, it flung a sheet of gummy silk impartially over the tarantula and the man.

Burl fought against the descending shroud. He strove to thrust it away, futilely. Within minutes he was completely covered in a coarse silken fabric that hid even the light from his eyes. He and his enemy, the monstrous tarantula, were beneath the same covering. The tarantula moved feebly.

The shower ceased. The web-spider had decided they were helpless. Then Burl felt the cables of the web give slightly as the spider approached to sting and suck the juices from its prey.

The web yielded gently. Burl froze in an ecstasy of horror. But the tarantula still writhed in agony upon the spear piercing it. It clashed its jaws, shuddering upon the horny shaft.

Burl waited for the poison-fangs to be thrust into him. He knew the process. He had seen the leisurely fashion in which the web-spider delicately stung its victim, then withdrew to wait with horrible patience for the poison to take effect. When the victim no longer struggled, it drew near again to suck out the juices first from one joint or limb and then from another, leaving a creature once vibrant with life a shrunken, withered husk, to be flung from the web at nightfall.

The bloated monstrosity now moved meditatively about the double object swathed in silk. Only the tarantula stirred. Its bulbous abdomen stirred the concealing shroud. It throbbed faintly as it still struggled with the spear in its vitals. The irregularly rounded projection was an obvious target for the web-spider. It moved quickly forward. With fine, merciless precision, it stung.

The tarantula seemed to go mad with pain. Its legs struck out purposelessly, in horrible gestures of delirious suffering. Burl screamed as a leg touched him. He struggled no less wildly.

His arms and head were enclosed by the folds of silk, but not glued to it because of the grease. Clutching at the cords he tried desperately to draw himself away from his deadly neighbor. The threads wouldn't break, but they did separate. A tiny opening appeared.

One of the tarantula's horribly writhing legs touched him again. With a strength born of utter panic he hauled himself away and the opening enlarged. Another lunge and Burl's head emerged into the open air. He was suspended twenty feet above the ground, which was almost carpeted with the chitinous remains of past victims of this same web.

Burl's head and breast and arms were free. The fish slung over his shoulder had shed its oil upon him impartially. But the lower part of his body was held firm by the viscous gumminess of the web-spider's cord. It was vastly more adhesive than any bird-lime ever made by men.

He hung in the little window for a moment, despairing. Then he saw the bulk of his captor a little distance away, waiting patiently for its poison to work and its prey to cease struggling. The tarantula was no more than shuddering now. Soon it would be quite still and the black-bellied creature would approach for its meal.

Burl withdrew his head and thrust desperately at the sticky stuff about his loins and legs. The oil upon his hands kept them free. The silk shroud gave a little. Burl grasped at the thought as at a straw. He grasped the fish and tore it, pushing frantically at his own body with the now-rancid, scaly, odorous mass. He scraped gum from his legs with the fish, smearing the rancid oils all over them in the process.

He felt the web tremble again. To the spider Burl's movements meant that its poison had not taken full effect. Another sting seemed necessary. This time it would not insert its sting into the quiescent tarantula, but where there was still life. It would send its venom into Burl.

He gasped and drew himself toward his window as if he would have pulled his legs from his body. His head emerged. His shoulders—half his body was out of the hole.

The great spider surveyed him and made ready to cast more of its silken stuff upon him. The spinnerets became active. A leg gathered it up—

The sticky stuff about Burl's feet gave way.

He shot out of the opening and fell heavily, sprawling upon the earth below and crashing into the shrunken shell of a flying beetle that had blundered into the snare and not escaped as he had done.

Burl rolled over and over and then sat up. An angry, foot-long ant stood before him, its mandibles extended threateningly, while a shrill stridulation filled the air.

In ages past, back on Earth—where most ants were to be measured in fractions of an inch—the scientists had debated gravely whether their tribe possessed a cry. They believed that certain grooves upon the body of the insect, like those upon the great legs of the cricket, might be the means of making a sound too shrill for human ears to catch. It was greatly debated, but evidence was hard to obtain.

Burl did not need evidence. He knew that the stridulation was caused by the insect before him, though he had never wondered how it was produced. The cry was emitted to summon other ants from its city to help it in difficulty or good fortune.

Harsh clickings sounded fifty or sixty feet away; comrades were coming. And while only army ants were normally dangerous, any tribe of ants could be formidable when aroused. It was overwhelming enough to pull down and tear a man to shreds as a pack of infuriated fox-terriers might do on Earth.

Burl fled without further delay, nearly colliding with

one of the web's anchor-cables. Then he heard the shrill outcry subside. The ant, short-sighted as all its kind, no longer
felt threatened. It went peacefully about the business Burl
had interrupted. Presently it found some edible carrion
among the debris from the spider-web and started triumphantly back to its city.

Burl sped on for a few hundred yards and then stopped.
He was shaken and dazed. For the moment, he was as timid
and fearful as any other man in his tribe. Presently he would
realize the full meaning of the unparalleled feat he had performed in escaping from the giant spider web while cloaked
with folds of gummy silk. It was not only unheard-of; it was
unimaginable! But Burl was too shaken to think of it now.

Rather quaintly, the first sensation that forced itself into
his consciousness was that his feet hurt. The gluey stuff
from the web still stuck to his soles, picking up small objects
as he went along. Old, ant-gnawed fragments of insect
armor pricked him so persistently, even through his tough-
ened foot-soles, that he paused to scrape them away, staring
fearfully about all the while. After a dozen stops more he
was forced to stop again.

It was this nagging discomfort, rather than vanity or an
emergency which caused Burl to discover—imagine—blunder into a new activity as epoch-making as anything else he
had done. His brain had been uncommonly stimulated in
the past twenty-some hours. It had plunged him into at least
one predicament because of his conceiving the idea of stabbing something, but it had also allowed him escape from
another even more terrifying one just now. In between it
had led to the devising of a purpose—the bringing of Saya
here—though that decision was not so firmly fixed as it had

been before the encounter with the web-spider. Still, it had surely been reasoning of a sort that told him to grease his body with the fish. Otherwise he would now be following the tarantula as a second course for the occupant of the web.

Burl looked cautiously all about him. It seemed to be quite safe. Then, quite deliberately, he sat down to think. It was the first time in his life that he had ever deliberately contemplated a problem with the idea of finding an answer to it. And the notion of doing such a thing was epoch-making—on this planet!

He examined his foot. The sharp edges of pebbles and the remnants of insect-armor hurt his feet when he walked. They had done so ever since he had been born, but never before had his feet been sticky, so that the irritation from one object persisted for more than a step. He carefully picked away each sharp-pointed fragment, one by one. Partly coated with the half-liquid gum, they even tended to cling to his fingers, except were the oil was thick.

Burl's reasoning had been of the simplest sort. He had contemplated a situation—not deliberately but because he had to—and presently his mind showed him a way out of it. It was a way specifically suited to the situation. Here he faced something different. Presently he applied the answer of one problem to a second problem. Oil on his body had let him go free of things that would stick to him. Here things stuck to his feet; so he oiled them.

And it worked. Burl strode away, almost—but not completely—untroubled by the bothersome pebbles and bits of discarded armor. Then he halted to regard himself with astonished appreciation. He was still thirty-five miles from his tribe; he was naked and unarmed, utterly ignorant of wood and fire and weapons other than the one he had lost. But he paused to observe with some awe that he was very wonderful indeed.

He wanted to display himself. But his spear was gone. So Burl found it necessary to think again. And the remarkable thing about it was that he succeeded.

In a surprisingly brief time he had come up with a list of answers. He was naked, so he would find garments for himself. He was weaponless: he would find himself a spear. He was hungry and he would seek food. Since he was far from his tribe, he would go to them. And this was, in a fashion, quite obviously thought; but it was not obvious on the forgotten planet because it had been futile—up to now. The importance of such thought in the scheme of things was that men had not been thinking even so simply as this, living only from minute to minute. Burl was fumbling his way into a habit of thinking from problem to problem. And that was very important indeed.

Even in the advanced civilization of other planets, few men really used their minds. The great majority of people depended on machines not only for computations but decisions as well. Any decisions not made by machines most men left to their leaders. Burl's tribesfolk thought principally with their stomachs, making few if any decisions on any other basis—though they did act, very often, under the spur of fear. Fear-inspired actions, however, were not thought out. Burl was thinking out his actions.

There would be consequences.

He faced upstream and began to move again, slowly and warily, his eyes keenly searching out the way ahead, ears alert for the slightest sound of danger. Gigantic butterflies, riotous in coloring, fluttered overhead through the hazy air.

Sometimes a grasshopper hurtled from one place to another like a projectile, its transparent wings beating frantically. Now and then a wasp sped by, intent upon its hunting, or a bee droned heavily alone, anxious and worried, striving to gather pollen in a nearly flowerless world.

Burl marched on. From somewhere far behind him came a very faint sound. It was a shrill noise, but very distant indeed. Absorbed in immediate and nearby matters, Burl took no heed. He had the limited local viewpoint of a child. What was near was important and what was distant could be ignored. Anything not imminent still seemed to him insignificant—and he was preoccupied.

The source of this sound was important, however. Its origin was a myriad clickings compounded into a single noise. It was, in fact, the far-away but yet perceptible sound of army ants on the march. The locusts of Earth were very trivial nuisances compared to the army ants of this planet.

Locusts, in past ages on Earth, had eaten all green things. Here in the lowlands were only giant cabbages and a few rank, tenacious growths. Grasshoppers were numerous here, but could never be thought of as a plague; they were incapable of multiplying to the size of locust hordes. Army ants, however. . . .

But Burl did not notice the sound. He moved forward briskly though cautiously, searching the fungus-landscape for any signs of garments, food, and weapons. He confidently expected to find all of them within a short distance. Indeed, he did find food very soon. No more than a half mile ahead he found a small cluster of edible fungi.

With no special elation, Burl broke off a food supply from the largest of them. Naturally, he took more than he could possibly eat at one time. He went on, nibbling at a big piece of mushroom abstractedly, past a broad plain, more than a mile across and broken into odd little hillocks by gradually ripening mushrooms which were unfamiliar to him. In several places the ground had been pushed aside by rounded objects, only the tips showing. Blood-red hemispheres seemed to be forcing themselves through the soil, so they might reach the outer air. Careful not to touch any of them, Burl examined the hillocks curiously as he entered the plain. They were strange, and to Burl most strange things meant danger. In any event, he had two conscious purposes now. He wanted garments and weapons.

Above the plain a wasp hovered, dangling a heavy object beneath its black belly across which ran a single red band. It was the gigantic descendant of the hairy sand-wasp, differing only in size from its far-away, remote ancestors on Earth. It was taking a paralyzed gray caterpillar to its burrow. Burl watched it drop down with the speed and sureness of an arrow, pull aside a heavy, flat stone, and descend into the burrow with its caterpillar-prey momentarily laid aside.

It vanished underground into a vertical shaft dug down forty feet or more. It evidently inspected the refuge. Reappearing, it vanished into the hole again, dragging the gray worm after it. Burl, marching on over the broad plain that was spotted with some eruptive disease, did not know what passed below. But he did observe the wasp emerge again to scratch dirt and stones previously excavated laboriously back into the shaft until it was full.

The wasp had paralyzed a caterpillar, taken it into the ready-prepared burrow, laid an egg upon it, and sealed up the entrance. In time the egg would hatch into a grub barely the size of Burl's forefinger. And the grub, deep underground, would feed upon the living but helpless caterpillar until it waxed large and fat. Then it would weave itself a cocoon and sleep a long sleep, only to wake as a wasp and dig its way out to the open air.

Reaching the farther side of the plain, Burl found himself threading the aisles of a fungus forest in which the growths were misshapen travesties of the trees which could not live here. Bloated yellow limbs branched off from rounded swollen trunks. Here and there a pear-shaped puffball, Burl's height and half his height again, waited until a chance touch should cause it to shoot upward a curling puff of infinitely fine dust.

He continued to move with caution. There were dangers here, but he went forward steadily. He still held a great mass of edible mushroom under one arm and from time to time broke off a fragment, chewing it meditatively. But always his eyes searched here and there for threats of harm.

Behind him the faint, shrill outcry had risen only slightly in volume. It was still too far away to attract his notice. Army ants, however, were working havoc in the distance. By thousands and millions, myriads of them advanced across the fungoid soil. They clambered over every eminence. They descended into every depression. Their antennae waved restlessly. Their mandibles were extended threateningly. The ground was black with them, each one more than ten inches long.

A single such creature, armored and fearless as it was, could be formidable enough to an unarmed and naked man like Burl. The better part of discretion would be avoidance. But numbering in the thousands and millions, they were something which could not be avoided. They advanced steadily and rapidly; the chorus of shrill stridulations and clickings marking their progress.

Great, inoffensive caterpillars crawling over the huge cabbages heard the sound of their coming, but were too stupid to flee. The black multitudes blanketed the rank vegetables. Tiny, voracious jaws tore at the flaccid masses of greasy flesh.

The caterpillars strove to throw off their assailants by writhings and contortions—uselessly. The bees fought their entrance into the monster hives with stings and wing-beats. Moths took to the air in daylight with dazzled, blinded eyes. But nothing could withstand the relentless hordes of small black things that reeked of formic acid and left the ground behind them empty of all life.

Before the horde was a world of teeming life, where mushrooms and other fungi fought with thinning numbers of cabbages and mutant earth-weeds for a foothold. Behind the black multitude was—nothing. Mushrooms, cabbages, bees, wasps, crickets, grubs—every living thing that could not flee before the creeping black tide reached it was lost, torn to bits by tiny mandibles.

Even the hunting spiders and tarantulas fell before the black host. They killed many in their desperate self-defense, but the army ants could overwhelm anything—anything at all—by sheer numbers and ferocity. Killed or wounded ants served as food for their sound comrades. Only the web-spiders sat unmoved and immovable in their colossal snares, secure in the knowledge that their gummy webs could not be invaded along the slender supporting cables.

The Purple Hills

3

THE ARMY ANTS flowed over the ground like a surging, monstrous, inky tide. Their vanguard reached the river and recoiled. Burl was perhaps five miles away when they changed their course. The change was made without confusion, the leaders somehow communicating the altered line of march to those behind them.

Back on Earth, scientists had gravely debated the question of how ants conveyed ideas to each other. Honeybees, it was said, performed elaborate ritual dances to exchange information. Ants, it had been observed, had something less eccentric. A single ant, finding a bit of booty too big for it to manage alone, would return to its city to secure the help of others. From that fact men had deduced that a language of gestures made with crossed antennae must exist.

Burl had no theories. He merely knew facts, but he did know that ants could and did pass information to one another. Now, however, he moved cautiously along toward the sleeping-place of his tribe in complete ignorance of the black blanket of living creatures spreading over the ground behind him.

A million tragedies marked the progress of the insect army. There was a tiny colony of mining bees, their habits unchanged despite their greater size, here on the forgotten planet. A single mother, four feet long, had dug a huge gallery with some ten offshooting cells, in which she had laid her eggs and fed her grubs with hard-gathered pollen. The grubs had waxed fat and large, become bees, and laid eggs in their turn within the same gallery their mother had dug out for them.

Ten bulky insects now foraged busily to feed their grubs within the ancestral home, while the founder of the colony had grown draggled and wingless with the passing of time. Unable to bring in food herself, the old bee became the guardian of the hive. She closed the opening with her head, making a living barrier within the entrance. She withdrew only to grant admission or exit to the duly authorized members—her daughters.

The ancient concierge of the underground dwelling was at her post when the wave of army ants swept over. Tiny, evil-smelling feet trampled upon her and she emerged to fight with mandible and sting for the sanctity of her brood. Within moments she was a shaggy mass of biting ants. They rent and tore at her chitinous armor. But she fought on madly, sounding a buzzing alarm to the colonists yet within.

They came out, fighting as they came: ten huge bees, each four to five feet long and fighting with legs and jaws, with wing and mandible, and with all the ferocity of so many tigers. But the small ants covered them, snapping at their multiple eyes, biting at the tender joints in their armor—and sometimes releasing the larger prey to leap upon an injured comrade, wounded by the monster they battled together.

Such a fight, however, could have but one end. Struggle as the bees might, they were powerless against their unnumbered assailants. They were being devoured even as they fought. And before the last of the ten was down the underground gallery had been gutted both of the stored food brought by the adult defenders and the last morsels of what had been young grubs, too unformed to do more than twitch helplessly, inoffensively, as they were torn to shreds.

When the army ants went on there were left merely an empty tunnel and a few fragments of tough armor, unappetizing even to the ants.

Burl heard them as he meditatively inspected the scene of a tragedy of not long before. The rent and scraped fragments of a great beetle's shiny casing lay upon the ground. A greater beetle had come upon the first and slain him. Burl regarded the remains of the meal.

Three or four minims, little ants barely six inches long, foraged industriously among the bits. A new ant-city was to be formed and the queen lay hidden half a mile away. These were the first hatchlings. They would feed their younger kindred until they grew large enough to take over the great work of the ant-city. Burl ignored the minims. He searched for a weapon of some sort. Behind him the clicking, high-pitched roar of the horde of army ants increased in volume.

He turned away disgustedly. The best thing he could find in the way of a weapon was a fiercely-toothed hind-leg. When he picked it up an angry whine rose from the ground.

One of the minims had been struggling to detach a morsel of flesh from the leg-joint. Burl had snatched the tidbit from him.

The little creature was surely no more than half a foot long, but it advanced angrily upon Burl, shrilling a challenge. He struck with the beetle's leg and crushed the ant. Two of the other minims appeared, attracted by the noise the first had made. They discovered the crushed body of their fellow, unceremoniously dismembered it, and bore it away in triumph.

Burl went on, swinging the toothed limb in his hand. The sound behind him became a distant whispering, high-pitched and growing steadily nearer. The army ants swept into a mushroom forest and the yellow, umbrellalike growths soon swarmed with the black creatures.

A great bluebottle fly, shining with a metallic lustre, stood beneath a mushroom on the ground. The mushroom was infected with maggots which exuded a solvent pepsin that liquefied the firm white meat. They swam ecstatically in the liquid gruel, some of which dripped and dripped to the ground. The bluebottle was sipping the dark-colored liquid through its long proboscis, quivering with delight as it fed on the noisomeness.

Burl drew near and struck. The fly collapsed in a quivering heap. Burl stood over it for an instant and pondered.

The army ants were nearer, now. They swarmed down into a tiny valley, rushing into and through a little brook over which Burl had leaped. Since ants can remain underwater for a long time without drowning, the small stream was not even dangerous. Its current did sweep some of them away. A great many of them, however, clung together until they chocked its flow by the mass of their bodies, the main force marching across the bridge they constituted.

The ants reached a place about a quarter of a mile to the left of Burl's line of march, perhaps a mile from the spot where he stood over the dead bluebottle. There was an expanse of some acres in which the giant, rank cabbages had so far succeeded in their competition with the world of fungi. The pale, cross-shaped flowers of the cabbages formed food for many bees. The leaves fed numberless grubs and worms. Under the fallen-away dead foliage—single leaves were twenty feet across at their largest—crickets hid and fed.

The ant-army flowed into this space, devouring every living thing it encountered. A terrible din arose. The crickets hurtled away in erratic leapings. They shot aimlessly in any direction. More than half of them landed blindly in the carpeting of clicking black bodies which were the ants from whose vanguard they had fled. Their blind flight had no effect save to give different individuals the opportunity to seize them as they fell and instantly begin to devour them. As they were torn to fragments, horrible screamings reached Burl's ears.

A single such cry of agony would not have attracted Burl's attention. He lived in a world of nightmare horror. But a chorus of creatures in torment made him look up. This was no minor horror. Something wholesale was in progress. He jerked his head about to see what it was.

A wild stretch of sickly yellow fungus was interspersed here and there with a squat toadstool, or a splash of vivid color where one of the many rusts had found a foothold. To the left a group of branched fungoids clustered in silent mockery of a true forest. Burl saw the faded green of the cabbages.

With the sun never shining on the huge leaves save through the cloud-bank overhead, the cabbages were not vivid. There were even some mouldy yeasts of a brighter green and slime much more luridly tinted. Even so, the cabbages were the largest form of true vegetation Burl had ever seen. The nodding white cruciform flowers stood out plainly against the yellowish, pallid green of the leaves. But as Burl gazed at them, the green slowly became black.

Three great grubs, in lazy contentment, were eating ceaselessly of the cabbages on which they rested. Suddenly first one and then another began to jerk spasmodically. Burl saw that around each of them a rim of black had formed. Then black motes milled all over them.

The grubs became black—covered with biting, devouring ants. The cabbages became black. The frenzied contortions of the grubs told of the agonies they underwent as they were literally devoured alive. And then Burl saw a black wave appear at the nearer edge of the stretch of yellow fungus. A glistening, living flood flowed forward over the ground with a roar of clickings and a persistent overtone of shrill stridulations.

Burl's scalp crawled. He knew what this meant. And he did not pause to think. With a gasp of pure panic he turned and fled, all intellectual preoccupations forgotten.

The black tide came on after him.

He flung away the edible mushroom he had carried under his arm. Somehow, though, he clung to the sharp-toothed club as he darted between tangled masses of fungus, ignoring now the dangers that ordinarily called for vast caution.

Huge flies appeared. They buzzed about him loudly. Once he was struck on the shoulder by one of them—at least as large as his hand—and his skin torn by its swiftly vibrating wings.

He brushed it away and sped on. But the oil with which he was partly covered had turned rancid, now, and the fetid odor attracted them. There were half a dozen—then a dozen creatures the size of pheasants, droning and booming as they kept pace with his wild flight.

A weight pressed onto his head. It doubled. Two of the disgusting creatures had settled upon his oily hair to sip the stuff through their hairy feeding-tubes. Burl shook them off with his hand and raced madly on, his ears attuned to the sounds of the ants behind him.

That clicking roar continued, but in Burl's ears it was almost drowned out by the noise made by the halo of flies accompanying him. Their buzzing had deepened in pitch with the increase in size of all their race. It was now the note close to the deepest bass tone of an organ. Yet flies—though greatly enlarged on the forgotten planet—had not become magnified as much as some of the other creatures. There were no great heaps of putrid matter for them to lay their eggs in. The ants were busy scavengers, carting away the debris of tragedies in the insect world long before it could acquire the gamey flavor beloved of fly-maggots. Only in isolated spots were the flies really numerous. In such places they clustered in clouds.

Such a cloud began to form about Burl as he fled. It seemed as though a miniature whirlwind kept pace with him—a whirlwind composed of furry, revolting bodies and multi-faceted eyes. Fleeing, Burl had to swing his club before him to clear the way. Almost every stroke was interrupted by an impact against some thinly-armored body which collapsed with the spurting of reddish liquid.

Then an anguish as of red-hot iron struck upon Burl's back. One of the stinging flies had thrust its sharp-tipped proboscis into his flesh to suck the blood. Burl uttered a cry and ran full-tilt into the stalk of a blackened, draggled toadstool.

There was a curious crackling as of wet punk. The toadstool collapsed upon itself with a strange splashing sound. A great many creatures had laid their eggs in it, until now it was a seething mass of corruption and ill-smelling liquid.

When the toadstool crashed to the ground, it crumbled into a dozen pieces, spattering the earth for yards all about with stinking stuff in which tiny, headless maggots writhed convulsively.

The deep-toned buzzing of the flies took on a note of solemn satisfaction. They settled down upon this feast. Burl staggered to his feet and darted off again. Now he was nothing but a minor attraction to the flies, only three or four bothering to come after him. The others settled by the edges of the splashing fluid, quickly absorbed in an ecstasy of feasting. The few still hovering about his head, Burl killed—but he did not have to smash them all. The remaining few descended to feast on their fallen comrades twitching feebly at his feet.

He ran on and passed beneath the wide-spreading leaves of an isolated giant cabbage. A great grasshopper crouched on the ground, its tremendous radially-opening jaws crunching the rank vegetation. Half a dozen great worms ate steadily of the leaves that supported them. One had swung itself beneath an overhanging leaf—which would have thatched houses for men—and was placidly anchoring itself for the spinning of a cocoon in which to sleep the sleep of meta-morphosis.

A mile away, the great black tide of army ants advanced relentlessly. The great cabbage, the huge grasshopper, and all the stupid caterpillars on the leaves would presently be covered with small, black demons. The cocoon would never be spun. The caterpillars would be torn into thousands of furry fragments and devoured. The grasshopper would strike out with his terrific, unguided strength, crushing its assailants with blows of its great hind-legs and powerful jaws. But it would die, making terrible sounds of torments as the ants consumed it piecemeal.

The sound of the ants' advance overwhelmed all other noises now. Burl ran madly, his breath coming in great gasps, his eyes wide with panic. Alone of the world about him, he knew the danger that followed him. The insects he passed went about their business with that terrifying, abstracted efficiency found only in the insect world.

Burl's heart pounded madly from his running. The breath whistled in his nostrils—and behind him the flood of army ants kept pace. They came upon the feasting flies. Some took to the air and escaped. Others were too absorbed in their delicious meal. The twitching maggots, stranded by the scattering of their soupy broth, were torn to shreds and eaten. The flies who were seized vanished into tiny maws. And the serried ranks of ants moved on.

Burl could hear nothing else, now, but the clickings of their limbs and the stridulating challenges and cross-challenges they uttered. Now and then another sound pierced the noises made by the ants themselves: a cricket, perhaps, seized and dying, uttering deep-bass cries of agony.

Before the horde there was a busy world which teemed

with life. Butterflies floated overhead on lazy wings; grubs waxed fat and huge; crickets feasted; great spiders sat quietly in their lairs, waiting with implacable patience for prey to fall into the trap-doors and snares; great beetles lumbered through the mushroom forests, seeking food and making love in monstrous, tragic fashion.

Behind the wide front of the army ants was—chaos. Emptiness. Desolation. All life save that of the army ants was exterminated, though some bewildered flying creatures still fluttered helplessly over the silent landscape. Yet even behind the army ants little bands of stragglers from the horde marched busily here and there, seeking some trace of life that had been overlooked by the main body.

Burl put forth his last ounce of strength. His limbs trembled. His breathing was agony. Sweat stood out upon his forehead. He ran for his life with the desperation of one who knows that death is at his heels. He ran as if his continued existence among the million tragedies of the single day were the purpose for which the universe had been created.

There was redness in the west and in the cloud-bank overhead. To the east gray sky became a deeper gray—much deeper. It was not yet time for the creatures of the day to seek their hiding-places, nor for the night-insects to come forth. But in many secret spots there were vague and sleepy stirrings.

Heedless of the approaching darkness Burl sped over an open space a hundred yards across. A thicket of beautifully golden mushrooms barred his way. Danger lay there. He dodged aside and saw in the gray dusk a glistening sheet of white, barely a yard above the ground. It was the web of the morning-spider which, on Earth, was noted only in hedges and such places when the dew of earliest dawn exposed it as a patternless plate of diamond-dust. There were anchor-cables, of course, but no geometry. Tidy housewives—also on Earth—used to mop it out of corners as a filmy fabric of irritating gossamer. On the forgotten planet it was a net with strength and birdlime qualities that increased day by day, as its spinner moved restlessly over the surface, always trailing sticky cord behind itself.

Burl had no choice but to avoid it, even though he lost ground to the ant-horde roaring behind him. And night was definitely on the way. It was inconceivable that a human should travel in the lowlands after dark. It literally could not be done over the normal nightmare terrain. Burl had not only to escape the army ants, but find a hiding-place quickly if he was to see tomorrow's light. But he could not think so far ahead, just now.

He blundered through a screen of puffballs that shot dusty powder toward the sky. Ahead, a range of strangely colored hills came into view—purple, green, black and gold—melting into each other and branching off, inextric-ably mingled. They rose to a height of perhaps sixty or seventy feet. A curious grayish haze had gathered above them. It seemed to be a layer of thin vapor, not like mist or fog, clinging to certain parts of the hills, rising slowly to coil and gather into an indefinitely thicker mass above the ridges.

The hills themselves were not geological features, but masses of fungus that had grown and cannibalized, piling up upon themselves to the thickness of carboniferous vegeta-tion. Over the face of the hills grew every imaginable variety of yeast and mould and rust. They grew within and upon themselves, forming freakish conglomerations that piled up into a range of hills, stretching across the lunatic landscape for miles.

Burl blundered up the nearest slope. Sometimes the surface was a hard rind that held him up. Sometimes his feet sank—perhaps inches, perhaps to mid-leg. He scrambled frantically. Panting, gasping, staggering from the exhaustion of moving across the fungus quicksand, he made his way to the top of the first hill, plunged down into a little valley on the farther side, and up another slope. He left a clear trail behind him of disturbed and scurrying creatures that had inevitably found a home in the mass of living stuff. Small sinuous centipedes scuttled here and there, roused by his passage. At the bottom of his footprints writhed fat white worms. Beetles popped into view and vanished again. . . .

A half mile across the range and Burl could go no farther. He stumbled and fell and lay there, gasping hoarsely. Overhead the gray sky had become a deep-red which was rapidly melting into that redness too deep to be seen except as black. But there was still some light from the west.

Burl sobbed for breath in a little hollow, his sharp-toothed club still clasped in his hands. Something huge, with wings like sails, soared in silhouette against the sunset. Burl lay motionless, breathing in great gasps, his limbs refusing to lift him.

The sound of the army ants continued. At last, above the crest of the last hillock he had surmounted, two tiny glistening antennae appeared, then the small, deadly shape of an army ant. The forerunner of its horde, it moved deliberately forward, waving its antennae ceaselessly. It made its way toward Burl, tiny clickings coming from its limbs.

A little wisp of vapor swirled toward the ant. It was the vapor that had gathered over the whole range of hills as a thin, low cloud. It enveloped the ant which seemed to be thrown into a strange convulsion, throwing itself about, legs moving aimlessly. If it had been an animal instead of an insect, it would have choked and gasped. But ants breathe through air-holes in their abdomens. It writhed helplessly on the spongy stuff across which it had been moving.

Burl was conscious of a strange sensation. His body felt remarkably warm. It felt hot. It was an unparalleled sensation, because Burl had no experience of fire or the heat of the sun. The only warmth he had ever known was when huddling together with his tribesmen in some hiding-place to avoid the damp chill of the night.

Then, the heat of their breath and flesh helped to combat discomfort. But this was a fiercer heat. It was intolerable. Burl moved his body with a tremendous effort and for a moment the fungus soil was cool beneath him. Then the sensation of hotness began again and increased until Burl's skin was reddened and inflamed.

The tenuous vapor, too, seemed to swirl his way. It made his lungs smart and his eyes water. He still breathed in painful gasps, but even that short period of rest had done him some good. But it was the heat that drove him to his feet again. He crawled painfully to the crest of the next hill. He looked back.

This was the highest hill he had come upon and he could see most of the purple range in the deep, deep dusk. Now he was more than half-way through the hills. He had barely a quarter-mile to go, northward. But east and west the range of purple hills was a ceaseless, undulating mass of lifts and hollows, of ridges and spurs of all imaginable colorings.

And at the tips of most of them were wisps of curling gray.

From his position he could see a long stretch of the hills not hidden by the surrounding darkness. Back along the way he had come, the army ants now swept up into the range of hills. Scouts and advance-guard parties scurried here and there. They stopped to devour the creatures inhabiting the surface layers. But the main body moved on inexorably.

The hills, though, were alive, not upheavals of the ground but festering heaps of insanely growing fungus, hollowed out in many places by tunnels, hiding-places, and lurking-places. These the ants invaded. They swept on, devouring everything. . . .

Burl leaned heavily upon his club and watched dully. He could run no more. The army ants were spreading everywhere. They would reach him soon.

Far to the right, the vapor thickened. A thin column of smoke arose in the dim half-light. Burl did not know smoke, of course. He could not conceivably guess that deep down in the interior of the insanely growing hills, pressure had killed and oxidation had carbonized the once-living material. By oxidation the temperature down below had been raised. In the damp darkness of the bowels of the hills spontaneous combustion had begun.

The great mounds of tinderlike mushroom had begun to burn very slowly, quite unseen. There had been no flames because the hills' surface remained intact and there was no air to feed the burning. But when the army ants dug ferociously for fugitive small things, air was admitted to tunnels abandoned because of heat.

Then slow combustion speeded up. Smoulderings became flames. Sparks became coals. A dozen columns of fume-laden smoke rose into the heavens and gathered into a dense pall above the range of purple hills. And Burl apathetically watched the serried ranks of army ants march on toward the widening furnaces that awaited them.

They had recoiled from the river instinctively. But their ancestors had never known fire. In the Amazon basin, on Earth, there had never been forest fires. On the forgotten planet there had never been fires at all, unless the first forgotten colonists tried to make them. In any case the army ants had no instinctive terror of flame. They marched into the blazing openings that appeared in the hills. They snapped with their mandibles at the leaping flames, and sprang to grapple with the burning coals.

The blazing areas widened as the purple surface was consumed. Burl watched without comprehension—even without thankfulness. He stood breathng more and more easily until the glow from approaching flames reddened his skin and the acrid smoke made tears fow from his eyes. Then he retreated slowly, leaning on his club and often looking back.

Night had fallen, but yet it was light to the army ants. They marched on, shrilling their defiance. They poured devotedly—and ferociously—into the inferno of flame. At last there were only small groups of stragglers from the great ant-army scurrying here and there over the ground their comrades had stripped of all life. The bodies of the main army made a vast malodor, burning in the furnace of the hills.

There had been pain in that burning, agony such as no

one would willingly dwell upon. But it came of the insane courage of the ants, attacking the burning stuff with their horny jaws, rolling over and over with flaming lumps of charcoal clutched in their mandibles. Burl heard them shrilling their war-cry even as they died. Blinded, antennae singed off, legs shriveling, they yet went forward to attack their impossible enemy.

Burl made his way slowly over the hills. Twice he saw small bodies of the vanished army. They had passed between the widening furnaces and furiously devoured all that moved as they forged ahead. Once Burl was spied, and a shrill cry was sounded, but he moved on and only a single ant rushed after him. Burl brought down his club and a writhing body remained to be eaten by its comrades when they came upon it.

And now the last faint traces of light had vanished in the west. There was no real brightness anywhere except the flames of the burning hills. The slow, slow nightly rain that dripped down all through the dark hours began. It made a pattering noise upon the unburnt part of the hills.

Burl found firm ground beneath his feet. He listened keenly for sounds of danger. Something rustled heavily in a thicket of toadstools a hundred feet away. There were sounds of preening, and of feet delicately placed here and there upon the ground. Then a great body took to the air with the throbbing beat of mighty wings.

A fierce down-current of air smote Burl, and he looked upward in time to glimpse the outline of a huge moth passing overhead. He turned to watch the line of its flight, and saw the fierce glow filling all the horizon. The hills burned brighter as the flames widened.

He crouched beneath a squat toadstool and waited for

the dawn. The slow-dropping rain kept on, falling with irregular, drumlike beats upon the tough top of the toadstool.

He did not sleep. He was not properly hidden, and there was always danger in the dark. But this was not the darkness Burl was used to. The great fires grew and spread in the masses of ready-carbonized mushroom. The glare on the horizon grew brighter through the hours. It also came nearer.

Burl shivered a little, as he watched. He had never even dreamed of fire before, and even the overhanging clouds were lighted by these flames. Over a stretch at least a dozen miles in length and from half a mile to three miles across, the seething furnaces and columns of flame-lit smoke sent illumination over the world. It was like the glow the lights of a city can throw upon the sky. And like the flitting of aircraft above a city was the assembly of fascinated creatures of the night.

Great moths and flying beetles, gigantic gnats and midges grown huge upon this planet, fluttered and danced above the flames. As the fire came nearer, Burl could see them: colossal, delicately formed creatures sweeping above the white-hot expanse. There were moths with riotously-colored wings of thirty-foot spread, beating the air with mighty strokes, their huge eyes glowing like garnets as they stared intoxicatedly at the incandescence below them.

Burl saw a great peacock-moth soaring above the hills with wings all of forty feet across. They fluttered like sails of unbelievable magnificence. And this was when all the separate flames had united to form a single sheet of white-hot burning stuff spread across the land for miles.

Feathery antennae of the finest lace spread out before the head of the peacock-moth; its body was of softest velvet.

A ring of snow-white fur marked where its head began. The glare from below smote the maroon of its body with a strange effect. For one instant it was outlined clearly. Its eyes shone more redly than any ruby's fire. The great, delicate wings were poised in flight. Burl caught the flash of flame upon the two great irridescent spots on the wings. Shining purple and bright red, all the glory of chalcedony and of chrysoprase was reflected in the glare of burning fungi.

And then Burl saw it plunge downward, straight into the thickest and fiercest of the leaping flames. It flung itself into the furnace as a willing, drunken victim of their beauty.

Flying beetles flew clumsily above the pyre also, their horny wing-cases stiffly outstretched. In the light from below they shone like burnished metal. Their clumsy bodies, with spurred and fierce-toothed limbs, darted through the flame-lit smoke like so many grotesque meteors.

Burl saw strange collisions and still stranger meetings. Male and female flying creatures circled and spun in the glare, dancing their dance of love and death. They mounted higher than Burl could see, drunk with the ecstasy of living, and then descended to plunge headlong in the roaring flames below.

From every side the creatures came. Moths of brightest yellow, with furry bodies palpitant with life, flew madly to destruction. Other moths of a deepest black, with gruesome symbols on their wings, swiftly came to dance above the glow like motes in sunlight.

And Burl crouched beneath a toadstool, watching while the perpetual, slow raindrops fell and fell, and a continuous hissing noise came from where the rain splashed amid the flames.

A Killer of Monsters

4

THE NIGHT WORE on, while the creatures above the firelight danced and died, their numbers ever reinforced by fresh arrivals. Burl sat tensely still, his eyes watching everything while his mind groped for an explanation of what he saw. At last the sky grew dimly gray, then brighter, and after a long time it was day. The flames of the burning hills seemed to dim and die as all the world became bright. After a long while Burl crawled from his hiding-place and stood erect.

No more than two hundred paces from where he stood, a straight wall of smoke rose from the still-smouldering fungus-range. Burl could see the smoke rising for miles on either hand. He turned to continue on his way, and saw the remains of one of the tragedies of the night.

A great moth had flown into the flames, been horribly scorched, and floundered out again. Had it been able to fly, it would have returned to its devouring deity; but now it lay upon the ground, its antennae hopelessly seared. One beautiful wing was nothing but gaping holes. The eyes had been dimmed by flame. The exquisitely tapering limbs lay broken and crushed by the violence of landing. The creature was helpless on the ground, only the stumps of its antennae moving restlessly and the abdomen pulsating slowly as it drew pain-racked breaths.

Burl drew near. He raised his club.

When he moved on there was a velvet cloak cast over his shoulders, gleaming with all the colors of the rainbows. A gorgeous mass of soft blue moth-fur was about his middle, and he had bound upon his forehead two yard-long fragments of the moth's magnificent antennae.

He strode on slowly, clad as no man had been clad in all the ages before him. After a while another victim of the holocaust—similarly blundered out to die—yielded him a spear that was longer and sharper and much more deadly than his first. So he took up his journey to Saya looking like a prince of Ind upon a bridal journey—though surely no mere prince ever wore such raiment.

For many miles, Burl threaded his way through an extensive forest of thin-stalked toadstools. They towered high over his head, colorful, parasitic moulds and rusts all about their bases. Twice he came upon open glades where bubbling pools of green slime festered in corruption. Once he hid himself as a monster scarabeus beetle lumbered by three yards away, clanking like some mighty machine.

Burl saw the heavy armor and inward-curving jaws of the monster. He almost envied him his weapons. The time was not yet come, though, when Burl and his kind would hunt such giants for the juicy flesh within its armored limbs. Burl was still a savage, still ignorant, still essentially timid.

His only significant advance had been that where at first he had fled without reasoning, now he paused to see if he need flee.

He was a strange sight, moving through the shadowed lanes of the forest in his cloak of velvet. The fierce-toothed leg of a fighting beetle rested in a strip of sinew about his waist, ready for use. His new spear was taller than himself. He looked like a conqueror. But he was still a fearful and a feeble creature, no match for the monstrous creatures about him. He was weak—and in that lay his greatest hope. Because if he were strong, he would not need to think.

Hundreds of thousands of years before, his ancestors had been forced to develop brains as penalty for the lack of claws or fangs. Burl was sunk as low as any of them, but he had to combat more horrifying enemies, more inexorable dangers, and many times more crafty antagonists. His ancestors had invented knives and spears and flying missiles, but the creatures about Burl had weapons a thousand times more deadly than the ones that had defended the first humans.

The fact, however, simply put a premium on the one faculty Burl had which the insect world has not.

In mid-morning he heard a discordant, deep-bass bellow, coming from a spot not twenty yards from where he moved. He hid in panic, waiting for an instant, listening.

The bellow came again, but this time with a querulous note. Burl heard a crashing and plunging as of some creature caught in a snare. A mushroom tumbled with a spongelike sound, and the thud was followed by a tremendous commotion. Something was fighting desperately against something else, but Burl did not know what creatures were in combat.

He waited, and the noise died gradually away. Presently his breath came more slowly and his courage returned. He stole from his hiding-place and would have made away, but new curiosity held him back. Instead of creeping from the scene, he moved cautiously toward the source of the noise.

Peering between two cream-colored stalks he saw a wide, funnel-shaped snare of silk spread out before him, some twenty yards across and as many deep. The individual threads could be plainly seen, but in the mass it seemed a fabric of sheerest, finest texture. Held up by tall mushrooms, it was anchored to the ground below and drew away to a small point through which a hole led to some as yet unseen recess. All the space of the wide snare was hung with threads: fine, twisted threads no more than half the thickness of Burl's finger.

This was the trap of a labyrinth spider. Not one of the interlacing strands was strong enough to hold any but the feeblest prey, but the threads were there by thousands. A cricket had become entangled in the sticky maze. Its limbs thrashed out and broke threads with every stroke, but each time became entangled in a dozen more. It struggled mightily, emitting at intervals—again—its horrible bass roar.

Burl breathed more easily. He watched with fascinated eyes. Mere death among insects—even tragic death—held no great interest for him. It was too common an occurrence. And there were few insects which deliberately sought man. Most insects have their allotted prey and will seek no others.

But this involved a spider, and spiders have a terrifying impartiality. A spider devouring some luckless insect was but an example of what might happen to Burl. So he watched alertly, his eyes traveling from the enmeshed cricket to the strange opening at the back of the funnel-shaped labyrinth.

That opening darkened. Two shining, glistening eyes had been watching from the tunnel in which the spider had been waiting. Now it swung out lightly, revealing itself as a gray spider, with twin black ribbons upon its thorax and two stripes of curiously speckled brown and white upon its abdomen. Burl saw, also, two curious appendages like a tail, as it came nimbly out of its hiding-place and approached the trapped creature.

The cricket was struggling weakly, now, and the cries it uttered were but feeble, because of the cords that fettered its limbs. Burl saw the spider throw itself upon the cricket which gave one final, convulsive shudder as fangs pierced its armor.

Shortly after, the spider fed. With bestial enjoyment it sucked all the succulence, all the fluid, from its victim's carcass.

Then the breath left Burl in a peculiar, frightened gasp. It was not from anything he saw or heard. It was something that he thought.

For a second, his knees knocked together in self-induced panic. It occurred to him that he, Burl, had killed a hunting spider—a tarantula—upon the red-clay cliff. True, the killing had been an accident and had nearly cost him his own life in the web-spider's snare. But—he had killed a spider and of the most deadly kind. Now it occurred to Burl that he could kill another.

Spiders were the ogres of the human tribes on the forgotten planet. Knowledge of them was hard to come by, because to study them was death. But all men knew that

web-spiders never left their traps. Never! And Burl had imagined himself making an impossibly splendid, incredibly
daring use of that fact.

Denying to himself that he intended any action so suicidal, he nevertheless drew back from the front of the snare
and made his way to the back, where the spider's tunnel was
no more than ten feet away.

Then he found himself waiting.

Presently, through the interstices of the silk, he saw the
gray bulk of the spider. It had left the drained and shrunken
carcass of the cricket to return to its resting-place, settling
itself carefully upon the soft walls of the fabric tunnel. From
the yielding, globular nest at the tunnel's end it fixed maniacal eyes once more upon the threads of its snare, seen down
the length of the passage-way.

Burl's hair stood on end from sheer fright, but he was
the slave of an idea.

The tunnel and the nest at its end did not rest on the
ground, but were suspended in air by cables like those that
spread the gin itself. The gray labyrinth-spider bulged the
fabric. It lay in luxurious comfort, waiting for victims to approach.

There was sweat on Burl's face as he raised his spear.
The bare idea of attacking a spider was horrifying. But actually he was in no danger whatever before the instant of the
spear-thrust, because web-spiders never, never, leave their
webs to hunt.

So Burl sweated, and grasped his spear with agonized
firmness—and thrust it into the bulge that was the spider's
body in its nest. He thrust with hysterical fury.

And then he ran as if the devil were after him.

It was a long time before he dared come back, his heart in his throat. All was still. He had missed the horrid convulsions of the wounded spider; he had not heard the frightful gnashings of its fangs at the piercing weapon, nor seen the silken threads of the tunnel ripped and torn in the spider's death-struggle. Burl came back to quietness. There was a great rent in the silken tunnel, and a puddle of ill-smelling stuff lay upon the ground. From time to time another droplet fell from the spear to join it. And the great spider had fallen half through its own enlargement of the rent made by the spear in the wall of the nest.

Burl stared. Even when he saw it, the thing was not easy to believe. The dead eyes of the spider looked at him with mad, frozen malignity. The fangs were still raised to kill. The hairy legs were still braced as if to enlarge further the gaping hole through which it had partly fallen.

Then Burl felt exultation. His tribe had been furtive vermin for almost forty generations, fleeing from the mighty insects, hiding from them, and when caught waiting helplessly for death, screaming shrilly in horror. But he, Burl, had turned the tables. He, a man, had killed a spider! His breast expanded. Always his tribesmen went quietly and fearfully, making no sound. But a sudden, surprising, triumphant yell burst from Burl's lips—the first hunting-cry of man upon the forgotten planet in two thousand years.

Next second, of course, his pulse almost stopped in sheer terror because he had made such a noise. He listened fearfully. The insect world was oblivious to him. Presently, shuddering but infinitely proud, he drew near his prey. He carefully withdrew his spear, poised to flee if the spider stirred. It did not. It was dead. The blood upon the spear was revolting. Burl wiped it off on a leathery toadstool. Then. . . .

He thought of Saya and his tribesmen. Trembling even as he gloated over his own remarkable self, he shifted the spider and worked it out of the nest. Presently he moved off with the belly of the spider upon his back and two of its hairy legs over his shoulders. The other limbs of the monster hung limp, trailing on the ground behind him.

Marching, then he was the first such spectacle in history. His velvet cloak shining with its irridescent spots, the yard-long scraps of golden antennae bound to his forehead, a spear in his hand, and the hideous bulk of a gray spider for burden—Burl was a very strange sight indeed.

He believed that other creatures fled before him because of the thing he carried. He tended to grow haughty. But actually, of course, insects do not know fear. They recognize their own specific enemies. That is necessary. But the life of the lowlands on the forgotten planet went on abstractedly, despite the splendid feat of one man.

Burl marched. He came upon a valley full of torn and tattered mushrooms. There was not a single yellow top among them. Every one had been infested with maggots that had liquefied the tough meat of the mushroom-tops, causing it to drip to the ground below. The liquid was gathered in a golden pool in the center of the small depression. Burl heard a loud and deep-toned humming before he saw the valley. Then he stopped and looked down.

He saw the golden pond, its surface reflecting the gray sky and the darkened stumps of mushrooms on the hillside which looked as if they had been blackened by a running flame. A small brooklet of golden liquid trickled over a rocky ledge, and all round the edges of the pond and brook, in ranks and rows, by hundreds and by thousands and it seemed by millions, were the green-gold bodies of great flies.

They were small compared to other insects. The flesh-flies laid their eggs by the hundreds in decaying carcasses. The others chose mushrooms to lay their eggs in. To feed the maggots that would hatch, a relatively great quantity of food was needed; therefore, the flies must remain comparatively small, or the body of a single grasshopper would furnish food for only a few maggots instead of the hundreds it must support. There must also be a limit to the size of worms if hundreds were to feast upon a single fungus.

But there was no limitation to the greediness of the adult creatures. There were bluebottles and green-bottles and all the flies of metallic lustre, gathered at a Lucullan feast of corruption. The buzzing of those swarming above the golden pool was a tremendous sound. The flying bodies flashed and glittered as they flew back and forth, seeking a place to alight and join in the orgy.

The glittering bodies clustered in already-found places were motionless as if carved from metal. Burl watched them. And then he saw motion overhead.

A slender, brilliant shape appeared, darting swiftly through the air, enlarging into a needle-like body with transparent, shining wings and two huge eyes. It circled and enlarged again, becoming a shimmering dragonfly, twenty feet and more in length. It poised itself abruptly above the pool, and then darted down, its jaws snapping viciously. They snapped again and again. Burl could not follow their slashings. And with each snap the glittering body of a fly vanished.

A second dragonfly appeared and a third. They swooped above the golden pool, snapping in mid-air, making their abrupt and angular turns, creatures of incredible ferocity and beauty. In that mass of buzzing creatures, even the most voracious appetite must soon have been sated, but the slender creatures still darted about in frenzied destruction.

And all this while the loud, contented, deep-bass humming went on as before. Their comrades were slaughtered by the hundreds not forty feet above their heads, but still the glittering rows of red-eyed flies gorged themselves upon the fluid of the pond. The dragonflies feasted until they were unable to devour even a single one more of their chosen prey. But even then they continued to sweep madly above the pool, striking down the buzzing flies though their bodies must perforce remain uneaten.

Some of the dead flies, crushed to pulp by the angry dragonflies, dropped among their feasting brothers. Presently, one of them placed its disgusting proboscis upon the mangled creature. It sipped daintily from the contents of the broken armor. Another joined it and another. In a little while a cluster of them pushed against each other for a chance to join them in a cannibalistic feast.

Burl turned aside and went on, leaving the dragonflies still at their massacre and the flies absorbed and ecstatic at their feast. The feast, indeed, was improved by the rain of murdered brethren from overhead.

Only a few miles farther on, Burl came upon a familiar landmark. He knew it well, but had always kept at a safe distance from it. A mass of rock had heaved itself up from the almost level plain over which he traveled to form an outjutting cliff. At one point the rock overhung, forming an inverted ledge—a roof over nothingness—which had been preempted by a hairy monster and made into a fairylike dwelling. A white hemisphere clung to the rock, firmly anchored by long cables.

Burl knew the place as one to be feared. A clotho spider had built itself a nest there, from which it emerged to hunt the unwary. Within the silken globe was a monstrosity, resting upon cushions of softest silk. The exterior had been beautiful once. But if one went too near one of the little inverted arches seemingly closed by panels of silk—it would open and out would rush a creature from a dream of hell.

Surely Burl knew this place. Hung upon the walls of the fairy palace were trophies. They had a purpose, of course. Stones and boulders hung there, too, to hold the structure firm against the storm-winds that rarely blew. But amid the stones and fragments of insect-armor there was a very special decoration: the shrunken, dessicated skeleton of a man.

The death of that man had saved Burl's life two years before. They had been together, seeking a new source of edible mushroom. The clotho spider was a hunter, not a spinner of webs. It had sprung suddenly from behind a great puffball as the two men froze in horror. Then it had come forward and deliberately chosen its victim. It did not choose Burl.

Now he looked with half-frightened speculation at the lair of his ancient enemy. Some day, perhaps. . . .

But now he passed on. He went past the thicket in which the great moths hid by day, past the slimy pool in which something unknown but terrible lurked. He penetrated the little forest of mushrooms that glowed at night and the place where the truffle-hunting beetles chirped thunderously during the dark hours.

And then he saw Saya. He caught a flash of pink skin vanishing behind a squat toadstool, and he ran forward calling her name. She emerged, and saw the figure with the horrible bulk of the spider on its back. She cried out in horror, and Burl understood. He let his burden fall, running swiftly to her.

They met. Saya waited timidly until she saw who this man was, and then she was astounded indeed. With golden plumes rising from his head, a velvet cloak about his shoulders, blue moth-fur about his middle, and a spear in his hand—and a dead spider behind him!—this was not the Burl she had known.

He took her hands, babbling proudly. She stared at him and at his victim—but the language of men had diminished sadly—struggling to comprehend. Presently her eyes glowed. She pulled at his wrists.

When they found the other tribesmen, they were carrying the dead spider between them, Saya looking more proud than Burl.

I N THEIR CLIMB up from savagery, the principal handicap from which men have always suffered is the fact that they are human. Or it can be said that human beings always have to struggle against the obstacle which is simply that they are men. To Burl his splendid return to the tribe called for a suitable reaction. He expected them to take note that he was remarkable, unparalleled, and in all ways admirable. He expected them to look at him with awe. He rather hoped that the sight of him would involve something like ecstasy.

And as a matter of fact, it did. For fully an hour. They gathered around him while he used his—and their—scanty vocabulary to tell them of his unique achievements and adventures during the past two days and nights. They listened attentively and with appropriate admiration and vicarious pride.

This in itself was a step upward. Mostly their talk was of where food might be found and where danger lurked. Strictly practical data connected with the pressing business of getting enough to eat and staying alive. The sheer pressure of existence was so great that the humans Burl knew had altogether abandoned such luxuries as boastful narrative. They had given up tradition. They did not think of art in even its most primitive forms, and the only craft they knew was the craftiness which promoted simple survival. So for them to listen to a narrative which did not mean either food or even a lessening of danger to themselves was a step upward on the cultural scale.

But they were savages. They inspected the dead spider, shuddering. It was pure horror. They did not touch it—the adults not at all, and even Dik and Tet not for a very long time. Nobody thought of spiders as food. Too many of them had been spiders' food.

But presently even the horror aroused by the spider palled. The younger children quailed at sight of it, of course; but the adults came to ignore it. Only the two gangling boys tried to break off a furry leg with which to charge and terrify the younger ones still further. They failed to get it loose because they did not think of cutting it. But they had nothing to cut it with anyhow.

Old Jon went wheezing off, foraging. He waved a hand to Burl as he went. Burl was indignant. But it was true that he had brought back no food. And people must eat.

Tama went off, her tongue clacking, with Lona the half-grown girl to help her find and bring back something edible. Dor, the strongest man in the tribe, went away to look where he thought there might be edible mushrooms full-grown again. Cori left with her children—very carefully on watch for danger to them—to see what she could find.

In a little more than an hour Burl's audience had diminished to Saya. Within two hours ants found the spider where it had been placed for the tribe to admire. Within three hours there was nothing left of it. During the fourth hour—as Burl struggled to dredge up some new, splendid item to tell Saya for the tenth time, or thereabouts—during the fourth hour one of the tribeswomen beckoned to Saya. She left with a flashing backward smile for Burl. She went, actually, to help dig up underground fungi—much like truffles—discovered by the older woman. She undoubtedly expected to share them with Burl.

But in five hours it was night and Burl was very indignant with his tribesfolk. They had shifted the location of the hiding-place for the night, and nobody had thought to tell him. And if Saya wished to come for Burl, to lead him to that place, she did not dare for the simple reason that it was night.

For a long time after he found a hiding-place, Burl fumed bitterly to himself. He was very much of a human being, differing from his fellows—so far—mainly because he had been through experiences not shared by them. He had resolved a subjective dilemma of sorts by determining to return to his tribe. He had discovered a weapon which, at first, had promised—and secured—foodstuff, and later had saved him from a tarantula. His discovery that fish-oil was useful when applied to spider-snares and things sticking to the feet was of vast importance to the tribe. Most remarkable of all, he had deliberately killed a spider. And he had experienced triumph. Temporarily he had even experienced admiration.

The adulation was a thing which could never be forgotten. Human appetites are formed by human experiences. One never had an appetite for a thing one has not known in

some fashion. But no human being who has known triumph
is ever quite the same again, and anybody who has once
been admired by his fellows is practically ruined for life—at
least so far as being independent of admiration is concerned.

So during the dark hours, while the slow rain dripped in
separate, heavy drops from the sky, Burl first coddled his
anger—which was a very good thing for a member of a race
grown timorous and furtive—and then began to make indignant plans to force his tribesmen to yield him more of
the delectable sensations he alone had begun to know.

He was not especially comfortable during the night.
The hiding-place he had chosen was not water-tight. Water
trickled over him for several hours before he discovered that
his cloak, though it would not keep him dry—which it
would have done if properly disposed—would still keep the
same water next to his skin where his body could warm it.
Then he slept. When morning came he felt singularly re-
freshed. For a savage, he was unusually clean, too.

He woke before dawn with vainglorious schemes in his
head. The sky grew gray and then almost white. The overhanging cloudbank seemed almost to touch the earth, but
gradually withdrew. The mist among the mushroom-forests
grew thinner, and the slow rain ceased reluctantly. When he
peered from his hiding-place, the mad world he knew was,
as far as he could see, quite mad, as usual. The last of the
night-insects had vanished. The day-creatures began to venture out.

Not too far from the crevice where he'd hidden was an
ant-hill, monstrous by standards on other planets. It was
piled up not of sand but gravel and small boulders. Burl saw
a stirring. At a certain spot the smooth, outer surface crum-

bled and fell into an invisible opening. A spot of darkness appeared. Two slender, threadlike antennae popped out. They withdrew and popped out again. The spot enlarged until there was a sizeable opening. An ant appeared, one of the warrior-ants of this particular breed. It stood fiercely over the opening, waving its antennae agitatedly as if striving to sense some danger to its metropolis.

He was fourteen inches long, this warrior, and his mandibles were fierce and strong. After a moment, two other warriors thrust past him. They ran about the whole extent of the ant-hill, their legs clicking, antennae waving restlessly.

They returned, seeming to confer with the first, then went back down into the city with every appearance of satisfaction. As if they made a properly reassuring report, within minutes afterward, a flood of black, ill-smelling workers poured out of the opening and dispersed about their duties.

The city of the ants had begun its daily toil. There were deep galleries underground here: graineries, storage-vaults, refectories, and nurseries, and even a royal apartment in which the queen-ant reposed. She was waited upon by assiduous courtiers, fed by royal stewards, and combed and caressed by the hands of her subjects and children. A dozen times larger than her loyal servants, she was no less industrious than they in her highly specialized fashion. From the time of her waking to the time of rest she was queen-mother in the most literal imaginable sense. At intervals, to be measured only in minutes, she brought forth an egg, perhaps three inches in length, which was whisked away to the municipal nursery. And this constant, insensate increase in the population of the city made all its frantic industry at once possible and necessary.

Burl came out and spread his cloak on the ground. In a little while he felt a tugging at it. An ant was tearing off a bit of the hem. Burl slew the ant angrily and retreated. Twice within the next half-hour he had to move swiftly to avoid foragers who would not directly attack him because he was alive—unless he seemed to threaten danger—but who lusted after the fabric of his garments.

This annoyance—and Burl would merely have taken it as a thing to be accepted a mere two days before—this annoyance added to Burl's indignation with the world about him. He was in a very bad temper indeed when he found old Jon, wheezing as he checked on the possibility of there being edible mushrooms in a thicket of poisonous, pink-and-yellow amanitas.

Burl haughtily commanded Jon to follow him. Jon's untidy whiskers parted as his mouth dropped open in astonishment. Burl's tribe was so far from being really a tribe that for anybody to give a command was astonishing. There was no social organization, absolutely no tradition of command. As a rule life was too uncertain for anybody to establish authority.

But Jon followed Burl as he stamped on through the morning mist. He saw a small movement and shouted imperatively. This was appalling! Men did not call attention to themselves! He gathered up Dor, the strongest of the men. Later, he found Jak who some day would wear an expression of monkey-like widsom. Then Tet and Dik, the half-grown boys, came trooping to see what was happening.

Burl led onward. A quarter of a mile and they came upon a great, gutted shell which had been a rhinoceros beetle the day before. Today it was a disassembled mass of chitinous armor. Burl stopped, frowning portentously. He showed his quaking followers how to arm themselves. Dor picked up the horn hesitantly, Burl showing him how to use it. He stabbed out awkwardly with the sharp fragment of armor. Burl showed others how to use the leg-sections for clubs. They tested them without conviction. In any sort of danger, they would trust to their legs and a frantically effective gift for hiding.

Burl snarled at his tribesmen and led them on. It was unprecedented. But because of that fact there was no precedent for rebellion. Burl led them in a curve. They glanced all about apprehensively.

When they came to an unusually large and attractive clump of golden edible mushrooms, there were murmurings. Old Jon was inclined to go and load himself and retire to some hiding-place for as long as the food lasted. But Burl snarled again.

Numbly they followed on—Dor and Jon and Jak and the two youngsters. The ground inclined upward. They came upon puffballs. There was a new kind visible, colored a lurid red, that did not grow like the others. It seemed to begin and expand underground, then thrust away the soil above in its development. Its taut, angry-red parchment envelope seemed to swell from a reservoir of subterranean material. Burl and the others had never seen anything like it.

They climbed higher. As other edible mushrooms came into view Burl's followers cheered visibly. This was a new tribal ground anyhow and it had not been fully explored. But Burl was leading them to quantities of food they had never suspected before.

Quaintly, it was Burl himself who began to feel an un-

comfortable dryness in his throat. He knew what he was
about. His followers did not suspect because to them what
he intended was simply inconceivable. They couldn't suspect it because they couldn't imagine anybody doing such a
thing. It simply couldn't be thought of at all.

It is rather likely that Burl began to regret that he had
thought of it. It had come to him first as an angry notion in
the night. Then the idea had developed as a suitable pun-
ishment for his abandonment. By dawn it was an ambition so terrifying that it fascinated him. Now he was committed to it in his own mind, and the only way to keep
his knees from knocking together was to keep moving. If his
followers had protested now, he would have allowed himself to be persuaded. But he heard more pleased murmurs.
There was more edible stuff, in quantity. But there were no
ant-trails here, no sounds of foraging beetles. This was an
area which Burl's tribesmen could clearly see was almost
devoid of dangerous life. They seemed to brighten a
little. This, they seemed to think, would be a good place
to move to.

But Burl knew better. There were few ground-insects
here because the area was hunted out. And Burl knew what
had done the hunting.

He expected the others to realize where they were when
they dodged around a clump of the new red puffballs and
saw bald rock before them and a falling-away to emptiness
beyond. Even then they could have retreated, but it did not
enter their heads that Burl could do anything like this.

They didn't know where they were until Burl held up
his hand for silence almost at the edge of the rock-knob
which rose a hundred feet sheer, curving out a little near its

top. They looked out uncomprehendingly at the mist-filled air and the nightmare landscape fading into its grayness. A tiny spider, the very youngest of hatchlings and barely four inches across, stealthily stalked another vastly smaller mite. The other was the many-legged larva of the oil-beetle. The larva itself had been called—on other planets by other men—the bee-louse. It could easily hide in the thick furl of a giant bumble-bee. But this one small creature never practiced that ability. The hatchling spider sprang and the small midge died. When the spider had grown and, being grown, spun a web, it would slay great crickets with the same insane ferocity.

Burl's followers saw first this and then certain three-quarter-inch strands of dirty silk that came up over the edge of the precipice. As one man after another realized where he was, he trembled violently. Dor turned gray. Jon and Jak were paralyzed with horror. They couldn't run.

Seeing the others even more frightened than himself filled Burl with a wholly unwarranted courage. When he opened his mouth, they cringed. If he shouted then at least one, more likely several, of them would die.

And this was because some forty or fifty feet down the mould-speckled precipice hung a drab-white object nearly hemispherical, some six feet in its half-diameter. A number of little semi-circular doors were fixed about its sides like arches. Though each one seemed to be a doorway, only one would open.

The thing had been oddly beautiful at first glance. It was held fast to the inward-sloping stone by cables, one or two of which stretched down toward the ground. Others reached up over the precipice-edge to hold it fast. It was a

most unusual engineering feat, yet something more than
that: this was also an ogre's castle. Ghastly trophies were
fastened to the outer walls and hung by silken cords below
it. Here was the hind-leg of one of the smaller beetles, there
the wing-case of a flying creature. Here a snail-shell—the
snails of Earth would hardly have recognized their descendant—and there a boulder weighing forty pounds or more.
The shrunken head-armor of a beetle, the fierce jaws of a
cricket, the pitiful shreds of dozens of creatures—all had
once provided meals for the monster in the castle. And dangling by the longest cord of all was the shrunken, shriveled
body of a long-dead man.

Burl glared at his tribesmen, clamping his jaws tight lest
they chatter. He knew, as did the others, that any noise
would bring the clotho spider swinging up its anchor-cables
to the cliff-top. The men didn't dare move. But every one of
them—and Burl was among the foremost—knew that inside
the half-dome of gruesome relics the monster reposed in
luxury and ease. It had eight furry, attenuated legs and a
face that was a mask of horror. The eyes glittered malevolently above needle-sharp mandibles. It was a hunting spider. At any moment it might leave the charnel-house in
which it lived to stalk and pursue prey.

Burl motioned the others forward. He led one of them
to the end of a cable where it curled up over the edge for an
anchorage. He ripped the end free—and his flesh crawled as
he did so. He found a boulder and knotted the end of the
cable about it. In a whisper that imitated a spider's ferocity,
Burl gave the man orders. He plucked a second quaking
tribesman by the arm. With the jerky, uncontrolled movements of a robot, Dor allowed himself to be led to a second
cable.

Burl commanded in a frenzy. He worked with stiff fingers and a dry throat, not knowing how he could do this thing. He had formed a plan in anger which he somehow was carrying out in a panic. Although his followers were as responsive as dead men, they obeyed him because they felt like dead men, unable to resist. After all, it was simple enough. There were boulders at the top of the precipice and silken cables hung taut over the edge. As Burl fastened a heavy boulder to each cable he could find, he loosened the silken strand until it hung tight only at the very edge of the more-than-vertical fall.

He took his post—and his followers gazed at him with the despairing eyes of zombies—and made a violent, urgent gesture. One man dumped his boulder over the precipice's edge. Burl cried out shrilly to the others, half-mad with his own terror. There was a ripping sound. The other men dumped their boulders over, fleeing with the movement—the paralysis of horror relieved by that one bit of exertion.

Burl could not flee. He panted and gasped, but he had to see. He stared down the dizzy wall. Boulders ripped and tore their way down the cliff-wall, pulling the cables loose from the face of the precipice. They shot out into space and jerked violently at the half-globular nest, ripping it loose from its anchorage.

Burl cried out exultantly. And as he cried out the shout became a bubbling sound; for although the ogre's silken castle did swing clear, it did not drop the sixty feet to the hard ground below. There was one cable Burl had missed, hidden by the rock-tripe and mould in a depressed part of the cliff-top. The spider's house was dangling crazily by that one strand, bobbing erratically to and fro in mid-air.

And there was a convulsive struggle inside it. One of the

arch-doors opened and the spider emerged. It was doubtless confused, but spiders simply do not know terror. There one response to the unusual is ferocity. There was still one cable leading up the cliff-face—the thing's normal climbing-rope to its hunting-ground above. The spider leaped for this single cable. Its legs grasped the cord. It swarmed upward, poison fangs unsheathed, mandibles clashing in rage. The shaggy hair of its body seemed to bristle with insane ferocity. The skinny articulated legs fairly twinkled as it rose. It made slavering noises, unspeakably horrifying.

Burl's followers were already in panic-stricken flight. He could hear them crashing through obstacles as they ran glassy-eyed from the horror they only imagined, but which Burl could not but encounter. Burl shivered, his body poised for equally frenzied but quite hopeless flight. But his first step was blocked. There was a boulder behind him, standing on end, reaching up to his knee. He could not take the first step without dodging it.

It was not the Burl of the terror-filled childhood who acted then. It was the throw-back, the atavism to a bolder ancestry. While the Burl who was a product of his environment was able to know only the stunned sensations of purest panic, the other Burl acted on a sounder basis of desperation. The emerging normal human seized the upright boulder. He staggered to the rock-face with it. He dumped it down the line of the descending cable.

Humans do have ancestral behavior-patterns built into their nervous systems. A frightened small child does not flee; it swarms up the nearest adult to be carried away from danger. At ten a child does not climb but runs. And there is an age when it is normal for a man to stand at bay. This last instinct can be conditioned away. In Burl's fellows and his immediate forbears it had been. But things had happened to Burl to break that conditioning.

He flung the pointed boulder down. For the fraction of a second he heard only the bubbling, gnashing sounds the spider made as it climbed toward him. Then there was a quite indescribable cushioned impact. After that, there were seconds in which Burl heard nothing whatever—and then a noise which could not be described either, but was the impact of the spider's body on the ground a hundred feet below, together with the pointed boulder it had fought insanely during all its fall. And the boulder was on top. The noise was sickening.

Burl found himself shaking all over. His every muscle was tense and strained. But the spider did not crawl over the edge of the precipice and something had hit far below.

A long minute later he managed to look.

The nest still dangled at the end of the single cable, festooned with its gruesome trophies. But Burl saw the spider. It was, of course, characteristically tenacious of life. Its legs writhed and kicked, but the body was crushed and mangled.

As Burl stared down, trying to breathe again, an ant drew near the shattered creature. It stridulated. Other ants came. They hovered restlessly at the edge of the death-scene. One loathsome leg did not quiver. An ant moved in on it.

The ants began to tear the dead spider apart, carrying its fragments to their city a mile away.

Up on the cliff-top Burl got unsteadily to his feet and found that he could breathe. He was drenched in sweat, but the shock of triumph was as overwhelming as any of the terrors felt by ancestors on this planet.

On no other planet in the Galaxy could any human experience such triumph as Burl felt now because never before had human beings been so completely subjugated by their environment. On no other planet had such an environment existed, with humans flung so helplessly upon its mercy.

Burl had been normal among his fellows when he was as frightened and furtive as they. Now he had been given shock treatment by fate. He was very close to normal for a human being newly come to the forgotten planet, save that he had the detailed information which would enable a normal man to cope with the nightmare environment. What he lacked now was the habit.

But it would be intolerable for him to return to his former state of mind.

He walked almost thoughtfully after his fled followers. And he was still a savage in that he was remarkably matter-of-fact. He paused to break off a huge piece of the edible golden mushrooms his fellow-men had noticed on the way up. Lugging it easily, he went back down over the ground that had looked so astonishingly free of inimical life—which it was because of the spider that had used it as a hunting-preserve.

Burl began to see that it was not satisfactory to be one of a tribe of men who ran away all the time. If one man with spear or stone could kill spiders, it was ridiculous for half a dozen men to run away and leave that one man the job alone. It made the job harder.

It occurred to Burl that he had killed ants without thinking too much about it, but nobody else had. Individual ants could be killed. If he got his followers to kill foot-long ants, they might in time battle the smaller, two-foot beetles.

If they came to dare so much, they might attack greater creatures and ultimately attempt to resist the real predators.

Not clearly but very dimly, the Burl who had been shocked back to the viewpoint which was normal to the race of men saw that human beings could be more than the fugitive vermin on which other creatures preyed. It was not easy to envision, but he found it impossible to imagine sinking back to his former state. As a practical matter, if he was to remain as leader his tribesmen would have to change.

It was a long time before he reached the neighborhood of the hiding-place of which he had not been told the night before. He sniffed and listened. Presently he heard faint, murmurous noises. He traced them, hearing clearly the sound of hushed weeping and excited, timid chattering. He heard old Tama shrilly bewailing fate and the stupidity of Burl in getting himself killed.

He pushed boldly through the toadstool-growth and found his tribe all gathered together and trembling. They were shaken. They chattered together—not discussing or planning, but nervously recalling the terrifying experience they had gone through.

Burl stepped through the screen of fungi and men gaped at him. Then they leaped up to flee, thinking he might be pursued. Tet and Dik babbled shrilly. Burl cuffed them. It was an excellent thing for him to do. No man had struck another man in Burl's memory. Cuffings were reserved for children. But Burl cuffed the men who had fled from the cliff-edge. And because they had not been through Burl's experiences, they took the cuffings like children.

He took Jon and Jak by the ear and heaved them out

of the hiding-place. He followed them, and then drove them to where they could see the base of the cliff from whose top they had tumbled stones—and then run away. He showed them the carcass of the spider, now being carted away piecemeal by ants. He told them angrily how it had been killed.

They looked at him fearfully.

He was exasperated. He scowled at them. And then he saw them shifting uneasily. There were clickings. A single, foraging black ant—rather large, quite sixteen inches long—moved into view. It seemed to be wandering purposelessly, but was actually seeking carrion to take back to its fellows. It moved toward the men. They were alive, therefore, it did not think of them as food—though it could regard them as enemies.

Burl moved forward and struck with his club. It was butchery. It was unprecedented. When the creature lay still he commanded one of his followers to take it up. Inside its armored legs there would be meat. He mentioned the fact, pungently. Their faces expressed amazed wonderment.

There was another clicking. Another solitary ant. Burl handed his club to Dor, pushing him forward. Dor hesitated. Though he was not afraid of one wandering ant, he held back uneasily. Burl barked at him.

Dor struck clumsily and botched the job. Burl had to use his spear to finish it. But a second bit of prey lay before the men.

Then, quite suddenly, this completely unprecedented form of foraging became understandable to Burl's followers. Jak giggled nervously.

An hour later Burl led them back to the tribe's hiding-place. The others had been terror-stricken, not knowing where the men had gone. But their terror changed to mute amazement when the men carried huge quantities of meat and edible mushroom into the hiding-place. The tribe held what amounted to a banquet.

Dik and Tet swaggered under a burden of ant-carcass. This was not, of course, in any way revolting. Back on Earth, even thousands of years before, Arabs had eaten locusts cooked in butter and salted. All men had eaten crabs and other crustaceans, whose feeding habits were similar to those of ants. If Burl and his tribesmen had thought to be fastidious, ants on the forgotten planet would still have been considered edible, since they had not lost the habits of extreme cleanliness which made them notable on Earth.

This feast of all the tribe, in which men had brought back not only mushroom to be eaten, but actual prey— small prey—of their hunting, was very probably the first such occasion in at least thirty generations of the forty-odd since the planet's unintended colonization. Like the other events, which began with Burl trying to spear a fish with a rhinoceros-beetle's horn, it was not only novel, on that world, but would in time have almost incredibly far-reaching consequences. Perhaps the most significant thing about it was its timing. It came at very nearly the latest instant at which it could have done any good.

There was a reason which nobody in the tribe would ever remember to associate with the significance of this banquet. A long time before—months in terms of Earthtime— there had been a strong breeze that blew for three days and nights. It was an extremely unusual windstorm. It had seemed the stranger, then, because during all its duration everyone in the tribe had been sick, suffering continuously.

When the windstorm had ended, the suffering ceased. A long time passed and nobody remembered it any longer.

There was no reason why they should. Yet, since that time there had been a new kind of thing growing among the innumerable moulds and rusts and toadstools of the lowlands. Burl had seen them on his travels, and the expeditionary force against the clotho spider had seen them on the journey up to the cliff-edge. Red puffballs, developing first underground, were now pushing the soil aside to expose taut, crimson parchment spheres to the open air. The tribesmen left them alone because they were strange; and strange things were always dangerous. Puffballs they were familiar with—big, misshappen things which shot at a touch a powder into the air. The particles of powder were spores —the seed from which they grew. Spores had remained infinitely small even on the forgotten planet where fungi grew huge. Only their capacity for growth had increased. The red growths were puffballs, but of a new and different kind.

As the tribe ate and admired, the hunters boasting of their courage, one of the new red mushrooms reached maturity.

This particular growing thing was perhaps two feet across, its main part spherical. Almost eighteen inches of the thing rose above-ground. A tawny and menacing red, the sphere was contained in a parchmentlike skin that was pulled taut. There was internal tension. But the skin was tough and would not yield, yet the inexorable pressure of life within demanded that it stretch. It was growing within, but the skin without had ceased to grow.

This one happened to be on a low hillside a good half-mile from the place where Burl and his fellows banqueted. Its tough, red parchment skin was tensed unendurably. Suddenly it ripped apart with an explosive tearing noise. The dry spores within billowed out and up like the smoke of a shell-explosion, spurting skyward for twenty feet and more. At the top of their ascent they spread out and eddied like a cloud of reddish smoke. They hung in the air. They drifted in the sluggish breeze. They spread as they floated, forming a gradually extending, descending dust-cloud in the humid air.

A bee, flying back toward its hive, droned into the thin mass of dust. It was preoccupied. The dust-cloud was not opaque, but only a thick haze. The bee flew into it.

For half a dozen wing-beats nothing happened. Then the bee veered sharply. Its deep-toned humming rose in pitch. It made convulsive movements in mid-air. It lost balance and crashed heavily to the ground. There its legs kicked and heaved violently but without purpose. The wings beat furiously but without rhythm or effect. Its body bent in paroxysmic flexings. It stung blindly at nothing.

After a little while the bee died. Like all insects, bees breathe through spiracles—breathing-holes in their abdomens. This bee had flown into the cloud of red dust which was the spore-cloud of the new mushrooms.

The cloud drifted slowly along over the surface of yeasts and moulds, over toadstools and variegated fungus monstrosities. It moved steadily over a group of ants at work upon some bit of edible stuff. They were seized with an affliction like that of the bee. They writhed, moved convulsively. Their legs thrashed about. They died.

The cloud of red dust settled as it moved. By the time it

had travelled a quarter-mile, it had almost all settled to the
ground.

But a half-mile away there was another skyward-spurt-
ing uprush of red dust which spread slowly with the breeze.
A quarter-mile away another plumed into the air. Farther
on, two of them spouted their spores toward the clouds almost together.

Living things that breathed the red dust writhed and
died. And the red-dust puffballs were scattered everywhere.

Burl and his tribesmen feasted, chattering in hushed
tones of the remarkable fact that men ate meat of their own
killing.

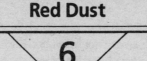

Red Dust

6

I T WAS VERY fortunate indeed that the feast took place
when it did. Two days later it would probably have been
impossible, and three days later it would have been too late
to do any good. But coming when it did, it made the difference which was all the difference in the world.

Only thirty hours after the feasting which followed the
death of the clotho spider, Burl's fellows—from Jon to Dor
to Tet and Dik and Saya—had come to know a numb despair which the other creatures of his world were simply a
bit too stupid to achieve.

It was night. There was darkness over all the lowlands,
and over all the area of perhaps a hundred square miles
which the humans of Burl's acquaintance really knew. He,
alone of his tribe, had been as much as forty miles from the
foraging-ground over which they wandered. At any given
time the tribe clung together for comfort, venturing only as
far as was necessary to find food. Although the planet possessed continents, they knew less than a good-sized county

of it. The planet owned oceans, and they knew only small brooks and one river which, where they knew it, was assuredly less than two hundred yards across. And they faced stark disaster that was not strictly a local one, but beyond their experience and hopelessly beyond their ability to face.

They were superior to the insects about them only in the fact that they realized what was threatening them.

The disaster was the red puffballs.

But it was night. The soft, blanketing darkness of a cloud-wrapped world lay all about. Burl sat awake, wrapped in his magnificent velvet cloak, his spear beside him and the yard-long golden plumes of a moth's antennae bound to his forehead for a headdress. About him and his tribesmen were the swollen shapes of fungi, hiding the few things that could be seen in the darkness. From the low-hanging clouds the nightly rain dripped down. Now a drop and then another drop; slowly, deliberately, persistently moisture fell from the skies.

There were other sounds. Things flew through the blackness overhead—moths with mighty wing-beats that sometimes sent rhythmic wind-stirrings down to the tribe in its hiding-place. There were the deep pulsations of sound made by night-beetles aloft. There were the harsh noises of grasshoppers—they were rare—senselessly advertising their existence to nearby predators. Not too far from where Burl brooded came bright chirrupings where relatively small beetles roamed among the mushroom-forests, singing cheerfully in deep bass voices. They were searching for the underground tidbits which took the place of the truffles their ancestors had lived on back on Earth.

All seemed to be as it had been since the first humans

were cast away upon this planet. And at night, indeed, the new danger subsided. The red puffballs did not burst after sunset. But Burl sat awake, brooding in a new sort of frustration. He and all his tribe were plainly doomed—yet Burl had experienced too many satisfying sensations lately to be willing to accept the fact.

The new red growths were everywhere. Months ago a storm-wind blew while somewhere, not too far distant, other red puffballs were bursting and sending their spores into the air. Since it was only a windstorm, there was no rain to wash the air clean of the lethal dust. The new kind of puffball—but perhaps it was not new: it could have thriven for thousands of years where it was first thrown as a sport from a genetically unstable parent—the new kind of puffball would not normally be spread in this fashion. By chance it had.

There were dozens of the things within a quarter-mile, hundreds within a mile, and thousands upon thousands within the area the tribe normally foraged in. Burl had seen them even forty miles away, as yet immature. They would be deadly at one period alone—the time of their bursting. But there were limitations even to the deadliness of the red puffballs, though Burl had not yet discovered the fact. But as of now, they doomed the tribe.

One woman panted and moaned in her exhausted sleep, a little way from where Burl tried to solve the problem presented by the tribe. Nobody else attempted to think it out. The others accepted doom with fatalistic hopelessness. Burl's leadership might mean extra food, but nothing could counter the doom awaiting them—so their thoughts seemed to run.

But Burl doggedly reviewed the facts in the darkness,

while the humans about him slept the sleep of those without hope and even without rebellion. There had been many burstings of the crimson puffballs. As many as four and five of the deadly dust-clouds had been seen spouting into the air at the same time. A small boy of the tribe had breathlessly told of seeing a hunting-spider killed by the red dust. Lana, the half-grown girl, had come upon one of the gigantic rhinoceros-beetles belly-up on the ground, already the prey of ants. She had snatched a huge, meat-filled joint and run away, faster than the ants could follow. A far-ranging man had seen a butterfly, with wings ten yards across, die in a dust-cloud. Another woman—Cori—had been nearby when a red cloud settled slowly over long, solid lines of black worker-ants bound on some unknown mission. Later she saw other workers carrying the dead bodies back to the ant-city to be used for food.

Burl still sat wakeful and frustrated and enraged as the slow rain fell upon the toadstools that formed the tribe's lurking-place. He doggedly went over and over the problem. There were innumerable red puffballs. Some had burst. The others undoubtedly would burst. Anything that breathed the red dust died. With thousands of the puffballs around them it was unthinkable that any human in this place could escape breathing the red dust and dying. But it had not always been so. There had been a time when there were no red puffballs here.

Burl's eyes moved restlessly over the sleeping forms limned by a patch of fox-fire. The feathery plumes rising from his head were outlined softly by the phosphorescence. His face was lined with a frown as he tried to think his own and his fellows' way out of the predicament. Without realizing it, Burl had taken it upon himself to think for his tribe. He had no reason to. It was simply a natural thing for him to do so, now that he had learned to think—even though his efforts were crude and painful as yet.

Saya woke with a start and stared about. There had been no alarm—merely the usual noises of distant murders and the songs of singers in the night. Burl moved restlessly. Saya stood up quietly, her long hair flowing about her. Sleepy-eyed, she moved to be near Burl. She sank to the ground beside him, sitting up—because the hiding-place was crowded and small—and dozed fitfully. Presently her head dropped to one side. It rested against his shoulder. She slept again.

This simple act may have been the catalyst which gave Burl the solution to his problem. Some few days before, Burl had been in a far-away place where there was much food. At the time he'd thought vaguely of finding Saya and bringing her to that place. He remembered now that the red puffballs flourished there as well as here—but there had been other dangers in between, so the only half-formed purpose had been abandoned. Now, though, with Saya's head resting against his shoulder, he remembered the plan. And then the stroke of genius took place.

He formed the idea of a journey which was not a going-after-food. This present dwelling-place of the tribe had been free of puffballs until only recently. There must be other places where there were no red puffballs. He would take Saya and his tribesmen to such a place.

It was really genius. The people of Burl's tribe had no purposes, only needs—for food and the like. Burl had achieved abstract thought—which previously had not been useful on the forgotten planet and, therefore, not practised. But it was time for humankind to take a more fitting place in the unbalanced ecological system of this nightmare world, time to change that unbalance in favor of humans.

When dawn came, Burl had not slept at all. He was all authority and decision. He had made plans.

He spoke sternly, loudly—which frightened people conditioned to be furtive—holding up his spear as he issued commands. His timid tribesfolk obeyed him meekly. They felt no loyalty to him or confidence in his decisions yet, but they were beginning to associate obedience to him with good things. Food, for one.

Before the day fully came, they made loads of the remaining edible mushroom and uneaten meat. It was remarkable for humans to leave their hiding-place while they still had food to eat, but Burl was implacable and scowling. Three men bore spears at Burl's urging. He brandished his long shaft confidently as he persuaded the other three to carry clubs. They did so reluctantly, even though previously they had killed ants with clubs. Spears, they felt, would have been better. They wouldn't be so close to the prey then.

The sky became gray over all its expanse. The indefinite bright area which marked the position of the sun became established. It was part-way toward the center of the sky when the journey began. Burl had, of course, no determined course, only a destination—safety. He had been carried south, in his misadventure on the river. There were red puffballs to southward, therefore he ruled out that direction. He could have chosen the east and come upon an ocean, but no safety from the red spore-dust. Or he could have chosen the north. It was pure chance that he headed west.

He walked confidently through the gruesome world of the lowlands, holding his spear in a semblance of readiness. Clad as he was, he made a figure at once valiant and rather pathetic. It was not too sensible for one young man—even one who had killed two spiders—to essay leading a tiny tribe of fearful folk across a land of monstrous ferocity and incredible malignance, armed only with a spear from a dead insect's armor. It was absurd to dress up for the enterprise in a velvety cloak made of a moth's wing, blue moth-fur for a loin-cloth, and merely beautiful golden plumes bobbing above his forehead.

Probably, though, that gorgeousness had a good effect upon his followers. They surely could not reassure each other by their numbers! There was a woman with a baby in her arms—Cori. Three children of nine or ten, unable to resist the instinct to play even on so perilous a journey, ate almost constantly of the lumps of food-stuff they had been ordered to carry. After them came Dik, a long-legged adolescent boy with eyes that roved anxiously about. Behind him were two men. Dor with a short spear and Jak hefting a club, both of them badly frightened at the idea of fleeing from dangers they knew and were terrified by, to other dangers unknown and, consequently, more to be feared. The others trailed after them. Tet was rear-guard. Burl had separated the pair of boys to make them useful. Together they were worthless.

It was a pathetic caravan, in a way. In all the rest of the Galaxy, man was the dominant creature. There was no other planet from one rim to the other where men did not build their cities or settlements with unconscious arrogance—completely disregarding the wishes of lesser things. Only on

this planet did men hide from danger rather than destroy it.
Only here could men be driven from their place by lower
life-forms. And only here would a migration be made on
foot, with men's eyes fearful, their bodies poised to flee at
sight of something stronger and more deadly than themselves.

They marched, straggling a little, with many waverings
aside from a fixed line. Once Dik saw the trapdoor of a trap-
door-spider's lair. They halted, trembling, and went a long
way out of their intended path to avoid it. Once they saw a
great praying-mantis a good half-mile off, and again they de-
viated from their proper route.

Near midday their way was blocked. As they moved onward, a great, high-pitched sound could be heard ahead of
them. Burl stopped; his face grew pinched. But it was only a
stridulation, not the cries of creatures being devoured. It was
a horde of ants by the thousands and hundreds of thousands, and nothing else.

Burl went ahead to scout. And he did it because he did
not trust anybody else to have the courage or intelligence to
return with a report, instead of simply running away if the
news were bad. But it happened to be the sort of action
which would help to establish his position as leader of his
tribe.

Burl moved forward cautiously and presently came to
an elevation from which he could see the cause of the tremendous waves of sound that spread out in all directions
from the level plain before him. He waved to his followers
to join him, and stood looking down at the extraordinary
sight.

When they reached his side—and Saya was first—the
spectacle had not diminished. For quite half a mile in either

direction the earth was black with ants. It was a battle of opposing armies from rival ant-cities. They snapped and bit at each other. Locked in viselike embraces, they rolled over and over upon the ground, trampled underfoot by hordes of their fellows who surged over them to engage in equally suicidal combat. There was, of course, no thought of surrender or of quarter. They fought by thousands of pairs, their jaws seeking to crush each other's armor, snapping at each other's antennae, biting at each other's eyes. . . .

The noise was not like that of army-ants. This was the agonizing sound of ants being dismembered while still alive. Some of the creatures had only one or two or three legs left, yet struggled fiercely to entangle another enemy before they died. There were mad cripples, fighting insanely with head and thorax only, their abdomens sheared away. The whining battle-cry of the multitude made a deafening uproar.

From either side of the battleground a wide path led back toward separate ant-cities which were invisible from Burl's position. These highways were marked by hurrying groups of ants—reinforcements rushing to the fight. Compared to the other creatures of this world the ants were small, but no lumbering beetle dared to march insolently in their way, nor did any carnivores try to prey upon them. They were dangerous. Burl and his tribesfolk were the only living things remaining near the battlefield—with one single exception.

That exception was itself a tribe of ants, vastly less in number than the fighting creatures, and greatly smaller in size as well. Where the combatants were from a foot to fourteen inches long, these guerilla-ants were no more than the third of a foot in length. They hovered industriously at the edge of the fighting, not as allies to either nation, but strictly on their own account. Scurrying among the larger, fighting ants with marvelous agility, they carried off piecemeal the bodies of the dead and valiantly slew the more gravely wounded for the same purpose.

They swarmed over the fighting-ground whenever the tide of battle receded. Caring nothing for the origin of the quarrel and espousing neither side, these opportunists busily salvaged the dead and still-living debris of the battle for their own purposes.

Burl and his followers were forced to make a two-mile detour to avoid the battle. The passage between bodies of scurrying reinforcements was a matter of some difficulty. Burl hurried the others past a route to the front, reeking of formic acid, over which endless regiments and companies of ants moved frantically to join in the fight. They were intensely excited. Antennae waving wildly, they rushed to the front and instantly flung themselves into the fray, becoming lost and indistinguishable in the black mass of fighting creatures.

The humans passed precariously between two hurrying battalions—Dik and Tet pausing briefly to burden themselves with prey—and hurried on to leave as many miles as possible behind them before nightfall. They never knew any more about the battle. It could have started over anything at all—two ants from the different cities may have disputed some tiny bit of carrion and soon been reinforced by companions until the military might of both cities was engaged. Once it had started, of course, the fighters knew whom to fight if not why they did so. The inhabitants of the two cities had different smells, which served them as uniforms.

But the outcome of the war would hardly matter. Not

to the fighters, certainly. There were many red mushrooms in this area. If either of the cities survived at all, it would be because its nursery-workers lived upon stored food as they tended the grubs until the time of the spouting red dust had ended.

Burl's folk saw many of the red puffballs burst during the day. More than once they came upon empty, flaccid parchment sacs. More often still they came upon red puffballs not yet quite ready to emit their murderous seed.

That first night the tribe hid among the bases of giant puffballs of a more familiar sort. When touched they would shoot out a puff of white powder resembling smoke. The powder was harmless fortunately and the tribe knew that fact. Although not toxic, the white powder was identical in every other way to the terrible red dust from which the tribe fled.

That night Burl slept soundly. He had been without rest for two days and a night. And he was experienced in journeying to remote places. He knew that they were no more dangerous than familiar ones. But the rest of the tribe, and even Saya, were fearful and terrified. They waited timorously all through the dark hours for menacing sounds to crash suddenly through the steady dripping of the nightly rain around them.

The second day's journey was not unlike the first. The following day, they came upon a full ten-acre patch of giant cabbages bigger than a family dwelling. Something in the soil, perhaps, favored vegetation over fungi. The dozens of monstrous vegetables were the setting for riotous life: great slugs ate endlessly of the huge green leaves—and things preyed on them; bees came droning to gather the pollen of the flowers. And other things came to prey on the predators in their turn.

There was one great cabbage somewhat separate from the rest. After a long examination of the scene, Burl daringly led quaking Jon and Jak to the attack. Dor splendidly attacked elsewhere, alone. When the tribe moved on, there was much meat, and everyone—even the children—wore loin-cloths of incredibly luxurious fur.

There were perils, too. On the fifth day of the tribe's journey Burl suddenly froze in stillness. One of the hairy tarantulas which lived in burrows with a concealed trap-door at ground level, had fallen upon a scarabeus beetle and was devouring it only a hundred yards ahead. The tribesfolk trembled as Burl led them silently back and around by a safe detour.

But all these experiences were beginning to have an effect. It was becoming a matter of course that Burl should give orders which others should obey. It was even becoming matter-of-fact that the possession of food was not a beautiful excuse to hide from all danger, eating and dozing until all the food was gone. Very gradually the tribe was developing the notion that the purpose of existence was not solely to escape awareness of peril, but to foresee and avoid it. They had no clear-cut notion of purpose as yet. They were simply outgrowing purposelessness. After a time they even looked about them with dim stirrings of an attitude other than a desperate alertness for danger.

Humans from any other planet, surely, would have been astounded at the vistas of golden mushrooms stretching out in forests on either hand and the plains with flaking surfaces given every imaginable color by the moulds and rusts and tiny flowering yeasts growing upon them. They would have been amazed by the turgid pools the journeying tribe came upon, where the water was concealed by a thick layer of slime through which enormous bubbles of foul-smelling gas rose to enlarge to preposterous size before bursting abruptly.

Had they been as ill-armed as Burl's folk, though, visitors from other planets would have been at least as timorous. Lacking highly specialized knowledge of the ways of insects on this world, even well-armed visitors would have been in greater danger.

But the tribe went on without a single casualty. They had fleeting glimpses of the white spokes of symmetrical spider-webs whose least thread no member of the tribe could break.

Their immunity from disaster—though in the midst of danger—gave them a certain all-too-human concentration upon discomfort. Lacking calamities, they noticed their discomforts and grew weary of continual traveling. A few of the men complained to Burl.

For answer, he pointed back along the way they had come. To the right a reddish dust-cloud was just settling, and to the rear rose another as they looked.

And on this day a thing happened which at once gave the complainers the rest they asked for, and proved the fatality of remaining where they were. A child ran aside from the path its elders were following. The ground here had taken on a brownish hue. As the child stirred up the surface mould with his feet, dust that had settled was raised up again. It was far too thin to have any visible color. But the child suddenly screamed, strangling. The mother ran frantically to snatch him up.

The red dust was no less deadly merely because it had settled to the ground. If a storm-wind came now—but they were infrequent under the forgotten planet's heavy bank of clouds—the fallen red dust could be raised up again and scattered about until there would be no living thing anywhere which would not gasp and writhe—and die.

But the child would not die. He would suffer terribly and be weak for days. In the morning he could be carried.

When night began to darken the sky, the tribe searched for a hiding-place. They came upon a shelf-like cliff, perhaps twenty or thirty feet high, slanting toward the line of the tribesmen's travel. Burl saw black spots in it—openings. Burrows. He watched them as the tribe drew near. No bees or wasps went in or out. He watched long enough to be sure.

When they were very close, he was certain. Ordering the others to wait, he went forward to make doubly sure. The appearance of the holes reassured him. Dug months before by mining-bees, gone or dead now, the entrances to the burrows were weathered and bedraggled. Burl explored, first sniffing carefully at each opening. They were empty. This would be shelter for the night. He called his followers, and they crawled into the three-foot tunnels to hide.

Burl stationed himself near the outer edge of one of them to watch for signs of danger. Night had not quite fallen. Jon and Dor, hungry, went off to forage a little way beyond the cliff. They would be cautious and timid, taking no risks whatever.

Burl waited for the return of his explorers. Meanwhile he fretted over the meaning of the stricken child. Stirred-up red dust was dangerous. The only time when there would be no peril from it would be at night, when the dripping rainfall of the dark hours turned the surface of this world into thin slime. It occurred to Burl that it would be safe to travel at night, so far as the red dust was concerned. He rejected the idea instantly. It was unthinkable to travel at night for innumerable other reasons.

Frowning, he poked his spear idly at a tumbled mass of tiny parchment cup-like things near the entrance of a cave. And instantly movement became visible. Fifty, sixty, a hundred infinitesimal creatures, no more than half an inch in length, made haste to hide themselves among the thimble-sized paperlike cups. They moved with extraordinary clumsiness and immense effort, seemingly only by contortions of their greenish-black bodies. Burl had never seen any creature progress in such a slow and ineffective fashion. He drew one of the small creatures back with the point of his spear and examined it from a safe distance.

He picked it up on his spear and brought it close to his eyes. The thing redoubled its frenzied movements. It slipped off the spear and plopped upon the soft moth-fur he wore about his middle. Instantly, as if it were a conjuring-trick, the insect vanished. Burl searched for minutes before he found it hidden deep in the long, soft hairs of his garment, resting motionless and seemingly at ease.

It was the larval form of a beetle, fragments of whose armor could be seen near the base of the clayey cliff-side. Hidden in the remnants of its egg-casings, the brood of minute things had waited near the opening of the mining-bee tunnel. It was their gamble with destiny when mining-bee grubs had slept through metamorphosis and come uncertainly out of the tunnel for the first time, that some or many of the larvae might snatch the instant's chance to fasten to the bees' legs and writhe upward to an anchorage in their fur. It happened that this particular batch of eggs had been laid after the emergence of the grubs. They had no possible chance of fulfilling their intended role as parasites on insects of the order hymenoptera. They were simply and matter-of-factly doomed by the blindness of instinct, which had caused them to be placed where they could not possibly survive.

On the other hand, if one or many of them had found a lurking-place, the offspring of their host would have been doomed. The place filled by oil-beetle larvae in the scheme of things is the place—or one of the places—reserved for creatures that limit the number of mining-bees. When a bee-louse-infested mining-bee has made a new tunnel, stocked it with honey for its young, and then laid one egg to float on that pool of nourishment and hatch and feed and ultimately grow to be another mining-bee—at that moment of egg-laying, one small bee-louse detaches itself. It remains zestfully in the provisioned cell to devour the egg for which the provisions were accumulated. It happily consumes those provisions and, in time, an oil-beetle crawls out of the tunnel a mining-bee so laboriously prepared.

Burl had no difficulty in detaching the small insect and casting it away, but in doing so he discovered that others had hidden themselves in his fur without his knowledge. He plucked them away and found more. While savages can be highly tolerant of vermin too small to be seen, they feel a peculiar revolt against serving as host to creatures of sensible size. Burl reacted violently—as once he had reacted to the discovery of a leech clinging to his heel. He jerked off his loin-cloth and beat it savagely with his spear.

When it was clean, he still felt a wholly unreasonable

sense of humiliation. It was not clearly thought out, of course. Burl feared huge insects too much to hate them. But that small creatures should fasten upon him produced a completely irrational feeling of outrage. For the first time in very many years or centuries a human being upon the forgotten planet felt that he had been insulted. His dignity had been assailed. Burl raged.

This was a highly desirable development among the inhabitants of this world. On other planets, rabbits are not capable of anger at men. Men had rated with rabbits here. When Burl became infuriated with insects he took another step toward what men elsewhere consider a normal attitude toward the cosmos about them.

But as he raged, a triumphant shout came from nearby. Jon and Dor were returning from their foraging, loaded down with edible mushroom. They, also, had taken a step upward toward the natural dignity of men. They had so far forgotten their terror as to shout in exultation at their find of food. Up to now, Burl had been the only man daring to shout. Now there were two others.

In his overwrought state this was also enraging. The result of hurt vanity on two counts was jealousy, and the result of jealousy was a crazy foolhardiness. Burl ground his teeth and insanely resolved to do something so magnificent, so tremendous, so utterly breathtaking that there could be no possible imitation by anybody else. His thinking was not especially clear. Part of his motivation had been provided by the oil-beetle larvae. He glared about him at the deepening dusk, seeking some exploit, some glamorous feat, to perform immediately, even in the night.

He found one.

I T WAS LATE dusk and the reddened clouds overhead were deepening steadily toward black. Dark shadows hung everywhere. The clay cliff cut off all vision to one side, but elsewhere Burl could see outward until the graying haze blotted out the horizon. Here and there, bees droned homeward to hive or burrow. Sometimes a slender, graceful wasp passed overhead, its wings invisible by the swiftness of their vibration.

A few butterflies lingered hungrily in the distance, seeking the few things they could still feast upon. No moth had wakened yet to the night. The cloud-bank grew more sombre. The haze seemed to close in and shrink the world that Burl could see.

He watched, raging, for the sight that would provide him with the triumph to end all triumphs among his followers. The soft, down-reaching fingers of the night touched here and there and the day ended at those spots. Then, from the heart of the deep redness to the west a flying creature came. It was a beautiful thing— a yellow emperor butterfly—flapping eastward with great sail-like velvet wings that seemed black against the sunset. Burl saw it sweep across the incredible sky, alight delicately, and disappear behind a mass of toadstools clustered so thickly they seemed nearly a hillock and not a mass of growing things.

Then darkness closed in completely, but Burl still stared where the yellow emperor had landed. There was that temporary, utter quiet when day-things were hidden and night-things had not yet ventured out. Fox-fire glowed. Patches of pale phosphorescence—luminous mushrooms—shone faintly in the dark.

Presently Burl moved through the night. He could imagine the yellow emperor in its hiding-place, delicately preening slender limbs before it settled down to rest until the new day dawned. He had noted landmarks, to guide himself. A week earlier and his blood would have run cold at the bare thought of doing what he did now. In mere cool-headed detachment he would have known that what he did was close to madness. But he was neither cool-headed nor detached.

He crossed the clear ground before the low cliff. But for the fox-fire beacons he would have been lost instantly. The slow drippings of rain began. The sky was dead black. Now was the time for night-things to fly, and male tarantulas to go seeking mates and prey. It was definitely no time for ad-venturing.

Burl moved on. He found the close-packed toadstools by the process of running into them in the total obscurity. He fumbled, trying to force his way between them. It could not be done; they grew too closely and too low. He raged at this impediment. He climbed.

This was insanity. Burl stood on spongy mushroom-stuff that quivered and yielded under his weight. Somewhere something boomed upward, rising on fast-beating wings into blackness. He heard the pulsing drone of four-inch mosquitos close by. He moved forward, the fungus support swaying, so that he did not so much walk as stagger over the close-packed mushroom heads. He groped before him with his spear and panted a little. There was a part of him which was bitterly afraid, but he raged the more furiously because if once he gave way even to caution, it would turn to panic.

Burl would have made a strange spectacle in daylight, gaudily clothed as he was in soft blue fur and velvet cloak, staggering over swaying insecurity, coddling ferocity in himself against the threat of fear.

Then his spear told him there was emptiness ahead. Something moved, below. He heard and felt it stirring the toadstool-stalks on which he stood.

Burl raised his spear, grasping it in both hands. He plunged down with it, stabbing fiercely.

The spear struck something vastly more resistant than any mushroom could be. It penetrated. Then the stabbed thing moved as Burl landed upon it, flinging him off his feet, but he clung to the firmly imbedded weapon. And if his mouth had opened for a yell of victory as he plunged down, the nature of the surface on which he found himself, and the kind of movement he felt, turned that yell into a gasp of horror.

It wasn't the furry body of a butterfly he had landed on; his spear hadn't pierced such a creature's soft flesh. He had leaped upon the broad, hard back of a huge, meat-eating,

nocturnal beetle. His spear had pierced not the armor, but
the leathery joint-tissue between head and thorax.

The giant creature rocketed upward with Burl clinging
to his spear. He held fast with an agonized strength. His
mount rose from the blackness of the ground into the many
times more terrifying blackness of the air. It rose up and
up. If Burl could have screamed, he would have done so,
but he could not cry out. He could only hold fast, glassy-
eyed.

Then he dropped. Wind roared past him. The great insect was clumsy at flying. All beetles are. Burl's weight and
the pain it felt made its flying clumsier still. There was a
semi-liquid crashing and an impact. Burl was torn loose and
hurled away. He crashed into the spongy top of a mushroom
and came to rest with his naked shoulder hanging halfway
over some invisible drop. He struggled.

He heard the whining drone of his attempted prey. It
rocketed aloft again. But there was something wrong with it.
With his weight applied to the spear as he was torn free,
Burl had twisted the weapon in the wound. It had driven
deeper, multiplying the damage of the first stab.

The beetle crashed to earth again, nearby. As Burl
struggled again, the mushroom-stalk split and let him gently
to the ground.

He heard the flounderings of the great beetle in the
darkness. It mounted skyward once more, its wing-beats no
longer making a sustained note. It thrashed the air irregularly and wildly.

Then it crashed again.

There was seeming silence, save for the steady drip-drip
of the rain. And Burl came out of his half-mad fear: he sud-

denly realized that he had slain a victim even more magnificent than a spider, because this creature was meat.

He found himself astonishedly running toward the spot where the beetle had last fallen.

But he heard it struggle aloft once more. It was wounded to death. Burl felt certain of it this time. It floundered in mid-air and crashed again.

He was within yards of it before he checked himself. Now he was weaponless, and the gigantic insect flung itself about madly on the ground, striking out with colossal wings and limbs, fighting it knew not what. It struggled to fly, crashed, and fought its way off the ground—ever more weakly—then smashed again into mushrooms. There it floundered horribly in the darkness.

Burl drew near and waited. It was still, but pain again drove it to a senseless spasm of activity.

Then it struck against something. There was a ripping noise and instantly the close, peppery, burning smell of the red dust was in the air. The beetle had floundered into one of the close-packed red puffballs, tightly filled with the deadly red spores. The red dust would not normally have been released at night. With the nightly rain, it would not travel so far or spread so widely.

Burl fled, panting.

Behind him he heard his victim rise one last time, spurred to impossible, final struggle by the anguish caused by the breathed-in red dust. It rose clumsily into the darkness in its death-throes and crashed to the ground again for the last time.

In time to come, Burl and his followers might learn to use the red-dust puffballs as weapons—but not how to spread them beyond their normal range. But now, Burl was frightened. He moved hastily sidewise. The dust would travel down-wind. He got out of its possible path.

There could be no exultation where the red dust was. Burl suddenly realized what had happened to him. He had been carried aloft an unknown though not-great distance, in an unknown direction. He was separated from his tribe, with no faintest idea how to find them in the darkness. And it was night.

He crouched under the nearest huge toadstool and waited for the dawn, listening dry-throated for the sound of death coming toward him through the night.

But only the wing-beats of night-fliers came to his ears, and the discordant notes of gray-bellied truffle beetles as they roamed the mushroom thickets, seeking the places beneath which—so their adapted instincts told them—fungoid dainties, not too much unlike the truffles of Earth, awaited the industrious miner. And, of course, there was that eternal, monotonous dripping of the rain-drops, falling at irregular intervals from the sky.

Red puffballs did not burst at night. They would not burst anyhow, except at one certain season of their growth. But Burl and his folk had so far encountered the over-hasty ones, bursting earlier than most. The time of ripeness was very nearly here, though. When day came again, and the chill dampness of the night was succeeded by the warmth of the morning, almost the first thing Burl saw in the gray light was a tall spouting of brownish-red stuff leaping abruptly into the air from a burst red parchmentlike sphere.

He stood up and looked anxiously all around. Here and there, all over the landscape, slowly and at intervals, the plumes of fatal red sprang into the air. There was nothing quite like it anywhere else. An ancient man, inhabiting Earth, mght have likened the appearance to that of a scattered and leisurely bombardment. But Burl had no analogy for them.

He saw something hardly a hundred yards from where he had hidden during the night. The dead beetle lay there, crumpled and limp. Burl eyed it speculatively. Then he saw something that filled him with elation. The last crash of the beetle to the ground had driven his spear deeply between the joints of the corselet and neck. Even if the red dust had not finished the creature, the spear-point would have ended its life.

He was thrilled once more by his superlative greatness. He made due note that he was a mighty slayer. He took the antennae as proof of his valor and hacked off a great barb-edged leg for meat. And then he remembered that he did not know how to find his fellow-tribesmen. He had no idea which way to go.

Even a civilized man would have been at a loss, though he would have hunted for an elevation from which to look for the cliff hiding-place of the tribe. But Burl had not yet progressed so far. His wild ride of the night before had been at random, and the chase after the wounded beetle no less dictated by chance. There was no answer.

He set off anxiously, searching everywhere. But he had to be alert for all the dangers of an inimical world while keeping, at the same time, an extremely sharp eye out for bursting red puffballs.

At the end of an hour he thought he saw familiar things. Then he recognized the spot. He had come back to the dead beetle. It was already the center of a mass of small black bodies which pulled and hacked at the tough armor, gnawing out great lumps of flesh to be carried to the nearest ant-city.

Burl set off again, very carefully avoiding any place that he recognized as having been seen that morning. Sometimes he walked through mushroom-thickets—dangerous places to be in—and sometimes over relatively clear ground colored exotically with varicolored fungi. More than once he saw the clouds of red stuff spurting in the distance. Deep anxiety filled him. He had no idea that there were such things as points of the compass. He knew only that he needed desperately to find his tribesfolk again.

They, of course, had given him up for dead. He had vanished in the night. Old Tama complained of him shrilly. The night, to them, meant death. Jon quaked watchfully all through it. When Burl did not come to the feast of mushroom that Jon and Dor had brought back, they sought him. They even called timidly into the darkness. They heard the throbbing of huge wings as a great creature rose desperately into the sky, but they did not associate that sound with Burl. If they had, they would have been instantly certain of his fate.

As it was, the tribe's uneasiness grew into terror which rapidly turned to despair. They began to tremble, wondering what they would do with no bold chieftain to guide them. He was the first man to command allegiance from others in much too long a period, on the forgotten planet, but the submission of his followers had been the more complete for its novelty. His loss was the more appalling. Burl had mistaken the triumphant shout of the foragers.

He'd thought it independence of him—rivalry. Actually, the men dared to shout only because they felt secure under his leadership. When they accepted the fact that he had vanished—and to disappear in the night had always meant death—their old fears and timidity returned. To them it was added despair.

They huddled together and whispered to one another of their fright. They waited in trembling silence through all the long night. Had a hunting-spider appeared, they would have fled in as many directions as there were people, and undoubtedly all would have perished. But day came again, and they looked into each other's eyes and saw the self-same fear. Saya was probably the most pitiful of the group. Her face was white and drawn beyond that of any one else.

They did not move when day brightened. They remained about the bee-tunnels, speaking in hushed tones, huddled together, searching all the horizon for enemies. Saya would not eat, but sat still, staring before her in numbed grief. Burl was dead.

Atop the low cliff a red puffball glistened in the morning light. Its tough skin was taut and bulging, resisting the pressure of the spores within. Slowly, as the morning wore on, some of the moisture that kept the skin stretchable dried. The parchmentlike stuff contracted. The tautness of the spore-packed envelope grew greater. It became insupportable.

With a ripping sound, the tough skin split across and a rush of the compressed spores shot skyward.

The tribesmen saw and cried out and fled. The red stuff drifted down past the cliff-edge. It drifted toward the humans. They ran from it. Jon and Tama ran fastest. Jak and Cori and the others were not far behind. Saya trailed, in her despair.

Had Burl been there, matters would have been different. He had already such an ascendancy over the minds of the others that even in panic they would have looked to see what he did. And he would have dodged the slowly drifting death-cloud by day, as he had during the night. But his followers ran blindly.

As Saya fled after the others she heard shrieks of fright to the left and ran faster. She passed by a thick mass of distorted fungi in which there was a sudden stirring and panic lent wings to her feet. She fled blindly, panting. Ahead was a great mass of stuff—red puffballs—showing here and there among great fanlike growths, some twelve feet high, that looked like sponges.

She fled past them and swerved to hide herself from anything that might be pursuing by sight. Her foot slipped on the slimy body of a shell-less snail and she fell heavily, her head striking a stone. She lay still.

Almost as if at a signal a red puffball burst among the fanlike growths. A thick, dirty-red cloud of dust shot upward, spread and billowed and began to settle slowly toward the ground again. It moved as it settled, flowing over the inequalities of the ground as a monstrous snail or leach might have done, sucking from all breathing creatures the life they had within them. It was a hundred yards away, then fifty, then thirty. . . .

Had any member of the tribe watched it, the red dust might have seemed malevolently intelligent. But when the edges of the dust-cloud were no more then twenty yards from Saya's limp body, an opposing breeze sprang up. It was

a vagrant, fitful little breeze that halted the red cloud and
threw it into some confusion, sending it in a new direction.
It passed Saya without hurting her, though one of its misty
tendrils reached out as if to snatch at her in slow-motion.
But it passed her by.

Saya lay motionless on the ground. Only her breast rose
and fell shallowly. A tiny pool of red gathered near her head.

Some thirty feet from where she lay, there were three
miniature toadstools in a clump, bases so close together that
they seemed but one. From between two of them, however,
two tufts of reddish thread appeared. They twinkled back
and forth and in and out. As if reassured, two slender antennae followed, then bulging eyes and a small, black body
with bright-red scalloped markings upon it.

It was a tiny beetle no more than eight inches long—a
sexton or burying-beetle. Drawing near Saya's body it scurried onto her flesh. It went from end to end of her figure in a
sort of feverish haste. Then it dived into the ground beneath
her shoulder, casting back a little shower of hastily dug dirt
as it disappeared.

Ten minutes later, another small creature appeared,
precisely like the first. Upon the heels of the second came a
third. Each made the same hasty examination and dived
under her unmoving form.

Presently the ground seemed to billow at a spot along
Saya's side and then at another. Ten minutes after the arrival of the third beetle, a little rampart had reared itself all
about Saya's body, following her outlines precisely. Then
her body moved slightly, in little jerks, seeming to settle
perhaps half an inch into the ground.

The burying-beetles were of that class of creatures

which exploited the bodies of the fallen. Working from below, they excavated the earth. When there was a hollow space below they turned on their backs and thrust up with their legs, jerking at the body until it sank into the space they had made ready. The process would be repeated until at last all their dead treasures had settled down below the level of the surrounding ground. The loosened dirt then fell in at the sides, completing the inhumation. Then, in the underground darkness, it was the custom for the beetles to feast magnificently, gorging themselves upon the food they had hidden from other scavengers—and of course rearing their young also upon its substance.

Ants and flies were rivals of these beetles and not infrequently the sexton-beetles came upon carrion after ants had taken their toll, and when it already swarmed with maggots. But in this case Saya was not dead. The fact that she still lived, though unconscious, was the factor that had given the sexton-beetles this splendid opportunity.

She breathed gently and irregularly, her face drawn with the sorrow of the night before, while the desperately hurrying beetles swarmed about beneath her body, channelling away the soil so she would sink lower and lower into it. She descended slowly, a half-inch by a half-inch. The bright-red tufts of thread appeared again and a beetle made its way to the open air. It moved hastily about, inspecting the progress of the work.

It dived below again. Another inch and, after a long time, another, were excavated.

Matters still progressed when Burl stepped out from a group of overshadowing toadstools and halted. He cast his eyes over the landscape and was struck by its familiarity. He

was, in fact, very near the spot he had left the night before
in that maniacal ride on the back of a flying beetle. He
moved back and forth, trying to account for the feeling of
recognition.

He saw the low cliff, then, and moved eagerly toward it,
passing within fifty feet of Saya's body, now more than half-
buried in the ground. The loose dirt around the outline of
her figure was beginning to topple in little rivulets upon her.
One of her shoulders was already half-screened from view.
Burl passed on, unseeing.

He hurried a little. In a moment he recognized his location exactly. There were the mining-bee burrows. There was
a thrown-away lump of edible mushroom, cast aside as the
tribesfolk fled.

His feet stirred up a fine dust, and he stopped short. A
red puffball had burst here. It fully accounted for the absence of the tribe, and Burl sweated in sudden fear. He
thought instantly of Saya. He went carefully to make sure.
This was, absolutely, the hiding place of the tribe. There
was another mushroom-fragment. There was a spear,
thrown down by one of the men in his flight. Red dust had
settled upon the spear and the mushroom-fragments.

Burl turned back, hurrying again, but taking care to disturb the dust no more than he could possibly help.

The little excavation into which Saya was sinking inch
by inch was not in his path. Her body no longer lay above
the ground, but in it. Burl went by, frantic with anxiety
about the tribe, but about Saya most of all.

Her body quivered and sank a fraction into the ground.
Half a dozen small streams of earth were tumbling upon
her. In minutes she would be wholly hidden from view.

Burl went to beat among the mushroom-thickets, in quest of the bodies of his tribesfolk. The could have staggered out of the red dust and collapsed beyond. He would have shouted, but the deep sense of loneliness silenced him. His throat ached with grief. He searched on. . . .

There was a noise. From a huge clump of toadstools—perhaps the very one he had climbed over the night—there came the sound of crashings and the breaking of the spongy stuff. Twin tapering antennae appeared, and then a monster beetle lurched into the open space, its ghastly mandibles gaping sidewise.

It was all of eight feet long and supported by six crooked, saw-toothed legs. Huge, multiple eyes stared with preoccupation at the world. It advanced deliberately with clankings and clashings as of a hideous machine. Burl fled on the instant, running directly away from it.

A little depression lay in the ground before him. He did not swerve, but made to jump over it. As he leaped he saw the color of bare flesh, Saya, limp and helpless, sinking slowly into the ground with tricklings of dirt falling down to cover her. It seemed to Burl that she quivered a little.

Instantly there was a terrific struggle within Burl. Behind him was the giant meat-eating beetle; beneath him was Saya whom he loved. There was certain death lurching toward him on evilly crooked legs—and the life he had hoped for lay in a shallow pit. Of course he thought Saya dead.

Perhaps it was rage, or despair, or a simple human madness which made him act otherwise than rationally. The things which raise humans above brute creation, however, are only partly reasonable. Most human emotions—especially the creditable ones—cannot be justified by reason, and very few heroic actions are based upon logical thought.

Burl whirled as he landed, his puny spear held ready. In his left hand he held the haunch of a creature much like the one which clanked and rattled toward him. With a yell of insane defiance—completely beyond justification by reason—Burl flung that meat-filled leg at the monster.

It hit. Undoubtedly, it hurt. The beetle seized it ferociously. It crushed it. There was meat in it, sweet and juicy.

The beetle devoured it. It forgot the man standing there, waiting for death. It crunched the leg-joint of a cousin or brother, confusing the blow with the missile that had delivered it. When the tidbit was finished it turned and lumbered off to investigate another mushroom thicket. It seemed to consider that an enemy had been conquered and devoured and that normal life could go on.

Then Burl stopped quickly, and dragged Saya from the grave the sexton-beetles had labored so feverishly to provide for her. Crumbled soil fell from her shoulders, from her face, and from her body. Three little eight-inch beetles with black and red markings scurried for cover in terrified haste. Burl carried Saya to a resting-place of soft mould to mourn over her.

He was a completely ignorant savage, save that he knew more of the ways of insects than anybody anywhere else— the Ecological Service, which had stocked this planet, not being excepted. To Burl the unconsciousness of Saya was as death itself. Dumb misery smote him, and he laid her down gently and quite literally wept. He had been beautifully pleased with himself for having slain one flying beetle. But for Saya's seeming death, he would have been almost unbearable with pride over having put another to flight. But now he was merely a broken-hearted, very human young man.

But a long time later Saya opened her eyes and looked about bewilderedly.

They were in considerable danger for some time after that, because they were oblivious to everything but each other. Saya rested in half-incredulous happiness against Burl's shoulder as he told her jerkily of his attempt on a night-bound butterfly, which turned out to be a flying beetle that took him aloft. He told of his search for the tribe and then his discovery of her apparently lifeless body. When he spoke of the monster which had lurched from the mushroom thicket, and of the desperation with which he had faced it, Saya looked at him with warm, proud eyes. But Burl was abruptly struck with the remarkable convenience of that discovery. If his tribesmen could secure an ample supply of meat, they might defend themselves against attack by throwing it to their attackers. In fact, insects were so stupid that almost any object thrown quickly enough and fast enough, might be made to serve as sacrifices instead of themselves.

A timid, frightened whisper roused them from their absorption. They looked up. The boy Dik stood some distance away, staring at them wide-eyed, almost convinced that he looked upon the living dead. A sudden movement on the part of either of them would have sent him bolting away. Two or three other bobbing heads gazed affrightedly from nearby hiding-places. Jon was poised for flight.

The tribe had come back to its former hiding-place simply as a way to reassemble. They had believed both Burl and

Saya dead, and they accepted Burl's death as their own doom. But now they stared.

Burl spoke—fortunately without arrogance—and Dik and Tet came timorously from their hiding-places. The others followed, the tribe forming a frightened half-circle about the seated pair. Burl spoke again and presently one of the bravest—Cori—dared to approach and touch him. Instantly a babble of the crude labial language of the tribe broke out. Awed exclamations and questions filled the air.

But Burl, for once, showed some common sense. Instead of a vainglorious recital, he merely cast down the long, tapering antennae of the flying-beetle. They looked, and recognized their origin.

Then Burl curtly ordered Dor and Jak to make a chair of their hands for Saya. She was weak from her fall and the loss of blood. The two men humbly advanced and obeyed. Then Burl curtly ordered the march resumed.

They went on, more slowly than on previous days, but none-the-less steadily. Burl led them across-country, marching in advance with a matter-of-fact alertness for signs of danger. He felt more confidence than ever before. It was not fully justified, of course. Jon now retrieved the spear he had discarded. The small party fairly bristled with weapons. But Burl knew that they were liable to be cast away as impediments if flight seemed necessary.

As he led the way Burl began to think busily in the manner that only leaders find necessary. He had taught his followers to kill ants for food, though they were still uneasy about such adventures. He had led them to attack great yellow grubs upon giant cabbages. But they had not yet faced any actual danger, as he had done. He must drive them to face something. . . .

The opportunity came that same day, in late afternoon. To westward the cloud-bank was barely beginning to show the colors that presage nightfall, when a bumblebee droned heavily overhead, making for its home burrow. The little, straggling group of marching people looked up and saw the scanty load of pollen packed in the stiff bristles of the bee's hind-legs. It sped onward heavily, its almost transparent wings mere blurs in the air.

It was barely fifty feet above the ground. Burl dropped his glance and tensed. A slender-waisted wasp was shooting upward from an ambush among the noisome fungi of this plain.

The bee swerved and tried to escape. The wasp over-hauled it. The bee dodged frantically. It was a good four feet in length,—as large as the wasp, certainly—but it was more heavily built and could not make the speed of which the wasp was capable. It dodged with less agility. Twice, in desperation, it did manage to evade the plunging dives of the wasp, but the third time the two insects grappled in midair almost over the heads of the humans.

They tumbled downward in a clawing, biting, tangle of bodies and legs. They hit the ground and rolled over and over. The bee struggled to insert her barbed sting in the more supple body of her adversary. She writhed and twisted desperately.

But there came an instant of infinite confusion and the bee lay on her back. The wasp suddenly moved with that ghastly skilled precision of a creature performing an incredible feat instinctively, apparently unaware that it is doing so.

The dazed bee was swung upright in a peculiarly artificial pose. The wasp's body curved, and its deadly, rapier-sharp sting struck. . . .

The bee was dead. Instantly. As if struck dead by lightning. The wasp had stung in a certain place in the neck-parts where all the nerve-cords pass. To sting there, the wasp had to bring its victim to a particular pose. It was precisely the trick of a *desnucador*, the butcher who kills cattle by severing the spinal cord. For the wasp's purposes the bee had to be killed in this fashion and no other.

Burl began to give low-toned commands to his followers. He knew what was coming next, and so did they. When the sequel of the murder began he moved forward, his tribesmen wavering after him. This venture was actually one of the least dangerous they could attempt, but merely to attack a wasp was a hair-raising idea. Only Burl's prestige plus their knowledge made them capable of it.

The second act of the murder-drama was gruesomeness itself. The pirate-wasp was a carnivore, but this was the season when the wasps raised young. Inevitably there was sweet honey in the half-filled crop of the bee. Had she arrived safely at the hive, the sweet and sticky liquid would have been disgorged for the benefit of bee-grubs. The wasp avidly set to work to secure that honey. The bee-carcass itself was destined for the pirate-wasp's own offspring, and that squirming monstrosity is even more violently carnivorous than its mother. The parent wasp set about abstracting the dead bee's honey, before taking the carcass to its young one, because honey is poisonous to the pirate-wasp's grub. Yet insects cannot act from solicitude or anything but instinct. And instinct must be maintained by lavish rewards.

So the pirate-wasp sought its reward—an insane, insatiable, gluttonous satisfaction in the honey that was poison to its young. The wasp rolled its murdered victim upon its back again and feverishly pressed on the limp body to force out the honey. And this was the reason for its precise manner of murder. Only when killed by the destruction of all nerve-currents would the bee's body be left limp like this. Only a bee killed in this exact fashion would yield its honey to manipulation.

The honey appeared, flowing from the dead bee's mouth. The wasp, in trembling, ghoulish ecstasy, devoured it as it appeared. It was lost to all other sights or sensations but its feast.

And this was the moment when Burl signalled for the attack. The tribesmen's prey was deaf and blind and raptured. It was aware of nothing but the delight it savored. But the men wavered, nevertheless, when they drew near. Burl was first to thrust his spear powerfully into the trembling body.

When he was not instantly destroyed the others took courage. Dor's spear penetrated the very vitals of the ghoul. Jak's club fell with terrific force upon the wasp's slender waist. There was a crackling, and the long, spidery limbs quivered and writhed. Then Burl struck again and the creature fell into two writhing halves.

They butchered it rather messily, but Burl noticed that even as it died, sundered and pierced with spears, its long tongue licked out in one last rapturous taste of the honey that had been its undoing.

Some time later, burdened with the pollen laden legs of the great bee, the tribe resumed its journey.

Now Burl had men behind him. They were still timid and prone to flee at the least alarm, but they were vastly more dependable than they had been. They had attacked and slain a wasp whose sting would have killed any of them. They had done battle under the leadership of Burl, whose spear had struck the first blow. They were sharers of his glory and, therefore, much more nearly like the followers of a chieftain ought to be.

Their new spirit was badly needed. The red puffballs were certainly no less numerous in the new territory the tribe traversed than in the territory they had left. And the season of their ripening was further advanced. More and more of the ground showed the deadly rime of settled death-dust. To stay alive was increasingly difficult. When the full spore-casting season arrived, it would be impossible. And that season could not be far away.

The very next day after the killing of the wasp, survival despite the red dust had begun to seen unimaginable. Where, earlier, one saw a red-dust cloud bursting here and there at intervals, on this day there was always a billowing mass of lethal vapor in the air. At no time was the landscape free of a moving mist of death. Usually there were three or four in sight at once. Often there were half a dozen. Once there were eight. It could be guessed that in one day more they would ripen in such monstrous numbers that anything which walked or flew or crawled must breathe in the spores and perish.

And that day, just at sunset, the tribe came to the top of a small rise in the ground. For an hour they had been marching and countermarching to avoid the suddenly billowing clouds of dust. Once they had been nearly hemmed in when three of the dull-red mists seemed to flow together, enclosing the three sides of a circle. They escaped then only by the most desperate of sprinting.

But now they came to the little hillock and halted. Before them stretched a plain, all of four miles wide, colored a brownish brick-red by the red puffballs. The tribe had seen mushroom forests—they had lived in them—and knew of the dangers that lurked there. But the plain before them was not simply dangerous; it was fatal. To right and left it stretched as far as the eye could see, but away on its farther edge Burl caught a glimpse of flowing water.

Over the plain itself a thin red haze seemed to float. It was simply a cloud of the deadly spores, dispersed and indefinite, but constantly replenished by the freshly bursting puffballs. While the tribesfolk stood and watched, thick columns of dust rose here and there and at the other place, too many to count. They settled again but left behind enough of the fine powder to keep a thin red haze over all the plain. This was a mass of literally millions of the deadly growths. Here was one place where no carnivorous beetles roamed and where no spiders lurked. There were nothing here but the sullen columns of dust and the haze that they left behind.

And of course it would be nothing less than suicide to try to go back.

A Flight Continues

8

B URL KEPT HIS people alive until darkness fell. He had assigned watchers for each direction and when flight was necessary the adults helped the children to avoid the red dust. Four times they changed direction after shrill-voiced warnings. When night settled over the plain they were forced to come to a halt.

But the puffballs were designed to burst by day. Stumbled into, they could split at any time, and the humans did hear some few of the tearing noises that denoted a spore-spout in the darkness. But after the slow nightly rain began they heard no more.

Burl led his people into the plain of red puffballs as soon as the rain had lasted long enough to wash down the red haze still hanging in the air and turn the fallen spores to mud.

It was an enterprise of such absolute desperation that very likely no civilized man would have tried it. There were no stars, for guidance, nor compasses to show the way.

There were no lights to enable them to dodge the deadly things they strove to escape, and there was no possibility of their keeping a straight course in the darkness. They had to trust to luck in perhaps the longest long-shot that humans ever accepted as a gamble.

Quaintly, they used the long antennae of a dead flying-beetle as sense-organs for themselves. They entered the red plain in a long single file, Burl leading the way with one of the two feathery whips extended before him. Saya helped him check on what lay in the darkness ahead, but made sure not to leave his side. Others trailed behind, hand in hand.

Progress was slow. The sky was utter blackness, of course, but nowhere in the lowlands is there an absolute black. Where fox-fire doesn't burn without consuming, there are mushrooms with glows of their own. Rusts sometimes shone faintly. Naturally there were no fireflies or glow-worms of any sort; but neither were there any living things to hunt the tiny tribe as it moved half-blindly in single file through the plain of red puffballs. Within half an hour even Burl did not believe he had kept to his original line. An hour later they realized despairingly that they were marching helplessly through puffballs which would make the air unbreathable at dawn. But they marched on.

Once they smelled the rank odor of cabbages. They followed the scent and came upon them, glowing palely with parasitic moulds on their leaves. And there were living things here: huge caterpillars eating and eating, even in the dark, against the time of metamorphosis. Burl could have cried out infuriatedly at them because they were—so he assumed—immune to the death of the red dust. But the red dust was all about, and the smell of cabbages was not the smell of life.

It could have been, of course. Caterpillars breathe like all insects at every stage of their development. But furry caterpillars breathe through openings which are covered over with matted fur. Here, that matted fur acted to filter the air. The eggs of the caterpillars had been laid before the puff-balls were ready to burst. The time of spore-bearing would be over before the grubs were butterflies or moths. These creatures were safe against all enemies—even men. But men groped and blundered in the darkness simply because they did not think to take the fur garments they wore and hold them to their noses to serve as gas-masks or air-filters. The time for that would come, but not yet.

With the docility of despair, Burl's tribe followed him through all the night. When the sky began to pale in the east, they numbly resigned themselves to death. But still they followed.

And in the very early gray light—when only the very ripest of the red puffballs spouted toward a still-dark sky— Burl looked harassedly about him and could have groaned. He was in a little circular clearing, the deadly red things all about him. There was not yet light enough for colors to appear. There was merely a vast stillness everywhere, and a mocking hint of the hot and peppery scent of death-dust— now turned to mud—all about him.

Burl drooped in bitter discouragement. Soon the misty dust-clouds would begin to move about; the reddish haze would form above all this space. . . .

Then, quite suddenly, he lifted his head and whooped. He had heard the sound of running water.

His followers looked at him with dawning hope. Without a word to them, Burl began to run. They followed hastily and quickened their pace when his voice came back in a

shout of triumph. In a moment they had emerged from the
tangle of fungus growths to stand upon the banks of a wide
river—the same river whose gleam Burl had seen the day
before, from the farther side of the red puffball plain.

Once before, Burl had floated down a river upon a
mushroom raft. That journey had been involuntary. He had
been carried far from his tribe and Saya, his heart filled with
desolation. But now he viewed the swiftly running current
with delight.

He cast his eyes up and down the bank. Here and there
it rose in a low bluff and thick shelf-fungi stretched out
above the water. They were adaptations of the fungi that
once had grown on trees and now fed upon the incredibly
nourishing earth-banks formed of dead growing things. Burl
was busy in an instant, stabbing the relatively hard growths
with his spear and striving to wrench them free. The tribesmen stared blankly, but at a snapped order they imitated
him.

Soon two dozen masses of firm, light fungus lay upon
the shore. Burl began to explain what they were for, but Dor
remonstrated. They were afraid to part from him. If they
might embark on the same fungus-raft, it would be a different matter. Old Tama scolded him shrilly at the thought of
separation. Jon trembled at the mere idea.

Burl cast an apprehensive glance at the sky. Day was
rapidly approaching. Soon the red puffballs would burst and
shoot their dust-clouds into the air. This was no time to
make stipulations. Then Saya spoke softly.

Burl made the suggested great sacrifice. He took the
gorgeous velvet cloak of moth-wing from his shoulder and
tore it into a dozen long, irregular pieces along the lines of

the sinews reinforcing it. He planted his spear upright in the largest raft, fastening the other cranky craft to it with the improvised lines.

In a matter of minutes the small flotilla of rafts bobbed in the stream. One by one, Burl settled the folk upon them with stern commands about movement. Then he shoved them out from the bank. The collection of uneasy, floating things moved slowly out from shore to where the current caught them. Burl and Saya sat on the same section of fungus, the other trustful but frightened tribespeople clustered timorously about.

As they began to move between the mushroom-lined banks of the river, and as the mist of night-time lifted from its surface, columns of red dust spurted sullenly upward on the plain. In the light of dawn the deadly red haze was forming once more over the puffball plain.

By that time, however, the unstable rafts were speeding down the river, bobbing and whirling in the stream, with wide-eyed people as their passengers gazing in wonderment at the shores.

Five miles downstream, the red growths became less numerous and other forms of fungus took their places. Moulds and rusts covered the ground as grass did on more favored planets. Toadstools showed their creamy, rounded heads, and there were malformed things with swollen trunks and branches mocking the trees that were never seen in these lowlands. Once the tribesmen saw the grisly bulk of a hunting-spider outlined on the river-bank.

All through the long day they rode the current, while the insect life that had been absent in the neighborhood of the death-plain became abundant again. Bees once more droned overhead, and wasps and dragonflies. Four-inch mosquitoes appeared, to be driven off with blows. Glittering beetles made droning or booming noises as they flew. Flies of every imaginable metallic hue flew about. Huge butterflies danced above the steaming land and running river in seeming ecstasy at simply being alive.

All the thousand-and-one forms of insect life flew and crawled and swam and dived where the people on the rafts could see them. Water-beetles came lazily to the surface to snap at other insects on the surface. The shell-covered boats of caddis-flies floated in the eddies and backwaters.

The day wore on and the shores flowed by. The tribesmen ate of their food and drank of the river. When afternoon came the banks fell away and the current slackened. The shores became indefinite. The river merged itself into a vast swamp from which came a continual muttering.

The water seemed to grow dark when black mud took the place of the clay that had formed its bed. Then there appeared floating green things which did not move with the flowing water. They were the leaves of the water-lilies that managed to survive along with cabbages and a very few other plants in the midst of a fungus world. Twelve feet across, any one of the green leaves might have supported the whole of Burl's tribe.

They became so numerous that only a relatively narrow, uncovered stream flowed between tens of acres of the flat, floating leaves. Here and there colossal waxen blossoms could be seen. Three men could hide in those enormous flowers. They exhaled an almost overpowering fragrance into the air.

And presently the muttering sound that had been heard

far away grew in volume to an intermittent deep-bass roar. It seemed to come from the banks on either side. It was the discordant croaking of frogs, eight feet in length, which lived and throve in this swamp. Presently the tribesfolk saw them: green giants sitting immobile upon the banks, only opening their huge mouths to croak.

Here in the swamps there was such luxuriance of insect life that a normal tribal hunting-ground—in which tribesmen were not yet accustomed to hunt—would seem like a desert by comparison. Myriads of little midges, no more than three or four inches across their wings, danced above the water. Butterflies flew low, seemingly enamoured of their reflections in the glassy water.

The people watched as if their eyes would become engorged by the strange new things they saw. Where the river split and split and divided again, there was nothing with which they were familiar. Mushrooms did not grow here. Moulds, yes. But there were cattails, with stalks like trees, towering thirty feet above the waterways.

After a long, long time though, the streams began to rejoin each other. Then low hills loomed through the thicker haze that filled the air here. The river flowed toward and through them. And here a wall of high mountains rose toward the sky, but their height could not be guessed. They vanished in the mist even before the cloud-bank swallowed them.

The river flowed through a river-gate, a water-gap in the mountains. While day still held fully bright, the bobbing rafts went whirling through a narrow pass with sheer walls that rose beyond all seeing in the mist. Here there was even some white water. Above it, spanning a chasm five hundred feet across, a banded spider had flung its web. The rafts floated close enough to see the spider, a monster even of its kind, its belly swollen to a diameter of yards. It hung motionless in the center of the snare as the humans swept beneath it.

Then the mountains drew back and the tribe was in a valley where, look as they might, there was no single tawny-red puffball from whose spreading range the tribesmen were refugees. The rafts grounded and they waded ashore while still the day held. And there was food here in plenty.

But darkness fell before they could explore. As a matter of precaution Burl and his folk found a hiding-place in a mushroom-thicket and hid until morning. The night-sounds were wholly familiar to them. The noise of katydids was louder than usual—the feminine sound of that name gives no hint of the sonorous, deep-toned notes the enlarged creatures uttered—and that implied more vegetation as compared with straight fungoid flora. A great many fireflies glowed in the darkness shrouding the hiding-place, indicating that the huge snails they fed on were plentiful. The snails would make very suitable prey for the tribesmen also. But men were not yet established in their own minds as predators.

They were, though, definitely no longer the furtive vermin they had been. They knew there were such things as weapons. They had killed ants for food and a pirate-wasp as an exercise in courage. To some degree they were acquiring Burl's own qualities. But they were still behind him—and he still had some way to go.

The next day they explored their new territory with a boldness which would have been unthinkable a few weeks before. The new haven was a valley, spreading out to a second swamp at its lower end. They could not know it, but beyond the swamp lay the sea. Exploring, because of strictly practical purposes and not for the sake of knowledge, they found a great trap-door in the earth, sure sign of the lair of a spider. Burl considered that before many days the monster would have to be dealt with. But he did not yet know how it could be done.

His people were rapidly becoming a tribe of men, but they still needed Burl to think for them. What he could not think out, so far, could not be done. But a part of the proof that they needed Burl to think for them lay in the fact that they did not realize it. They gathered facts about their environment. The nearest ant-city was miles away. That meant that they would encounter its scouting foragers rather than working-parties. The ant-city would be a source of small prey—a notion that would have been inconceivable a little while ago. There were numerous giant cabbages in the valley and that meant there were big, defenseless slugs to spear whenever necessary.

They saw praying-mantises—the adults were eighteen feet tall and as big as giraffes, but much less desirable neighbors—and knew that they would have to be avoided. But there were edible mushrooms on every hand. If one avoided spiders and praying-mantises and the meat-eating beetles; if one were safely hidden at night against the amorous male spiders who took time off from courtship to devour anything living that came their way; and if one lived at high-tension alertness, interpreting every sound as possible danger and every unknown thing as certain peril—then one could live quite comfortably in this valley.

For three days the tribesmen felt that they had found a sort of paradise. Jon had his belly full to burstng all day long.

Tet and Dik became skilled ant-hunters. Dor found a better spear and practiced thoughtfully with it.

There were no red puffballs here. There was food. Burl's folk could imagine no greater happiness. Even old Tama scolded only rarely. They surely could not conceive of any place where a man might walk calmly about with no danger at all of being devoured. This was paradise!

And it was a deplorable state of affairs. It is not good for human beings to feel secure and experience contentment. Men achieve only by their wants or through their fears. Back at their former foraging-ground, the tribe would never have emulated Burl with any passion so long as they could survive by traditional behavior. Before the menace of the red puffballs developed, he had brought them to the point of killing ants, with him present and ready to assist. They would have stayed at about that level. The red dust had forced their flight. During that flight they had achieved what was—compared to their former timidity—prodigies of valor.

But now they arrived at paradise. There was food. They could survive here in the fashion of the good old days before they learned the courage of desperation. They did not need Burl to keep them alive or to feed them. They tended to disregard him. But they did not disperse. Social grouping is an instinct in human beings as it is in cattle or in schools of fish. Also, when Burl was available there was a sense of pleasant confidence. He had gotten them out of trouble before. If more trouble came, he would get them out of it again. But why look for trouble?

Burl's tribesmen sank back into a contented lethargy. They found food and hid themselves until it was all consumed. A part of the valley was found where they were far enough from visible dangers to feel blissfully safe. When they did move, though still with elaborate caution, it was only to forage for food. And they did not need to go far because there was plenty of food. They slipped back. Happier than they had ever been, the foragers finally began to forget to take their new spears or clubs with them. They were furtive vermin in a particularly favorable environment.

And Burl was infuriated. He had known adulation. He was cherished, to be sure, but adulation no longer came his way. Even Saya. . . .

An ironically natural change took place in Saya. When Burl was a chieftain, she looked at him with worshipful eyes. Now that he was as other men, she displayed coquetry. And Burl was of that peculiarly direct-thinking sort of human being who is capable of leadership but not of intrigue. He was vain, of course. But he could not engage in elaborate maneuvers to build up a romantic situation. When Saya archly remained with the women of the tribe, he considered that she avoided him. When she coyly avoided speech with him, he angrily believed that she did not want his company.

When they had been in the valley for a week, Burl went off on a bitter journey by himself. Part of his motivation, probably, was a childish resentment. He had been the great man of the tribe. He was no longer so great because his particular qualities were not needed. And—perhaps with some unconscious intent to punish them for their lessened appreciation—he went off in a pet.

He still carried spear and club, but the grandeur of his costume had deteriorated. His cloak was gone. The moth-antennae he had worn bound to his forehead were now so draggled that they were ridiculous. He went off angrily to be rid of his fellows' indifference.

He found the upward slopes which were the valley's lateral boundaries. They promised nothing. He found a minor valley in which a labyrinth spider had built its shining snare. Burl almost scorned the creature. He could kill it if he chose, merely by stabbing it through the walls of its silken nest as it waited for unlucky insects to blunder into the intricate web. He saw praying-mantises. Once he came upon that extraordinary egg-container of the mantis tribe: a gigantic leaf-shaped mass of solidified foam, whipped out of some special plastic compound which the mantis secretes, and in which the eggs are laid.

He found a caterpillar wrapped in its thick cocoon and, because he was not foraging and not particularly hungry, he inspected it with care. With great difficulty he even broke the strand of silk that formed it, unreeling several feet in curiosity. Had he meditated, Burl would have seen that this was cord which could be used to build snares as spiders did. It could also be used to make defenses in which—if built strongly and well—even hunting-spiders might be tangled and dispatched.

But again he was not knowingly looking for things to be of use. He coddled his sense of injury against his tribe. He punished them by leaving them.

He encountered a four-foot praying-mantis that raised its saw-toothed forelimbs and waited immobile for him to come within reach. He had trouble getting away without a fight. His spear would have been a clumsy weapon against so slender a target and the club certainly not quick enough to counter the insect's lightning-like movements.

He was bothered. That day he hunted ants. The difficulty was mainly that of finding individual ants, alone, who could be slaughtered without drawing hordes of others into the fight. Before nightfall he had three of them—foot-long carcasses—slung at his belt. Near sunset he came upon another fairly recent praying-mantis hatchling. It was almost an ambush. The young monster stood completely immobile and waited for him to walk into its reach.

Burl performed a deliberate experiment—something that had not been done for a very long time on the forgotten planet. The small, grisly creature stood as high as Burl's shoulders. It would be a deadly antagonist. Burl tossed it a dead ant.

It struck so swiftly that the motion of its horrible forearms could not be seen. Then it ignored Burl, devouring the tidbit.

It was a discovery that was immediately and urgently useful.

On the second day of his aimless journey Burl saw something that would be even more deadly and appalling than the red dust had been for his kind. It was a female black hunting-spider, the so-called American tarantula. When he glimpsed the thing the blood drained from Burl's face.

As the monster moved out of sight Burl, abandoning any other project he might have intended, headed for the place his tribe had more or less settled in. He had news which offered the satisfaction of making him much-needed again, but he would have traded that pleasure ten hundred times over for the simple absence of that one creature from this valley. That female tarantula meant simply and specifically that the tribe must flee or die. This place was not paradise!

The entry of the spider into the region had preceded the arrival of the people. A giant, even of its kind, it had come across some pass among the mountains for reasons only it could know. But it was deadliness beyond compare. Its legs spanned yards. The fangs were needle-sharp and feet in length—and poisoned. Its eyes glittered with insatiable, insane blood-lust. Its coming was ten times more deadly to the humans—as to the other living creatures of the valley—than a Bengal tiger loosed in a human city would have been. It was bad enough in itself, but it brought more deadly disaster still behind it.

Bumping and bouncing behind its abdomen as it moved, fastened to its body by dirtied silken ropes, this creature dragged a burden which was its own ferocity many times multiplied. It was dragging an egg-bag larger than its body—which was feet in diameter. The female spider would carry this ghastly burden—cherishing it—until the eggs hatched. And then there would be four to five hundred small devils loose in the valley. From the instant of their hatching they would be as deadly as their parent. Though the offspring would be small—with legs spanning no more than a foot—their bodies would be the size of a man's fist and able to leap two yards. Their tiny fangs would be no less envenomed than their mother's. In stark, maniacal hatred of all other life they would at least equal the huge gray horror which had begot them.

Burl told his tribesmen. They listened, eyes large with fright but not quite afraid. The thing had not yet happened. When Burl insistently commanded that they follow him on a new journey, they nodded uneasily but slipped away. He could not gather the tribe together. Always there were members who hid from him—and when he went in search of them, the ones he had gathered vanished before he could return.

There were days of bright light and murder, and nights of slow rain and death in the valley. The great creatures under the cloud-bank committed atrocities upon each other and blandly dined upon their victims. Unthinkingly solicitous parents paralyzed creatures to be left living and helpless for their young to feed on. There were enormities of cruelty done in the matter-of-fact fashion of the insect world. To these things the humans were indifferent. They were uneasy, but like other humans everywhere they would not believe the worst until the worst arrived.

Two weeks after their coming to the valley, the worst was there. When that day came the first gray light of dawn found the humans in a shivering, terrified group in a completely suicidal position. They were out in the open—not hidden but in plain view. They dared not hide any more. The furry gray monster's brood had hatched. The valley seemed to swarm with small grey demons which killed and killed, even when they could not devour. When they encountered each other they fought in slavering fury and the victors in such duels dined upon their brethren. But always they hunted for more things to kill. They were literally maniacs—and they were too small and too quick to fight with spears or clubs.

So now, at daybreak, the humans looked about despairingly for death to come to them. They had spent the night in the open lest they be trapped in the very thickets that had formerly been their protection. They were in clear sight of the large gray murderer, if it should pass that way. And they did not dare to hide because of that ogreish creature's brood.

The monster appeared. A young girl saw it and cried

out chokingly. It had not seen them. They watched it leap upon and murder a vividly-colored caterpillar near the limit of vision in the morning-mist. It was in the tribe's part of the valley. Its young swarmed everywhere. The valley could have been a paradise, but it was doomed to become a charnel-house.

And then Burl shook himself. He had been angry when he left the tribe. He had been more angry when he returned and they would not obey him. He had remained with them, petulantly silent, displaying the offended dignity he felt and elaborately refusing to acknowledge any overtures, even from Saya. Burl had acted rather childishly. But his tribesmen were like children. It was the best way for him to act.

They shivered, too hopeless even to run away while the shaggy monster feasted a half-mile away. There were six men and seven women besides himself, and the rest were children, from gangling adolescents to one babe in arms. They whimpered a little. Then Saya looked imploringly at Burl—coquetry forgotten now. The others whimpered more loudly. They had reached that stage of despair, now, when they could draw the monster to them by blubbering in terror.

This was the psychological moment. Burl said dourly: "Come!"

He took Saya's hand and started away. There was but one direction in which any human being could think to move in this valley, at this moment. It was the direction away from the grisly mother of horrors. It happened to be the way up the valley wall. Burl started up that slope. Saya went with him.

Before they had gone ten yards Dor spoke to his wife. They followed Burl, with their three children. Five yards more, and Jak agitatedly began to bustle his family into movement. Old Jon, wheezing, frantically scuttled after Burl, and Cori competently set out with the youngest of her children in her arms and the others marching before her. Within seconds more, all the tribe was in motion.

Burl moved on, aware of his following, but ignoring it. The procession continued in his wake simply because it had begun to do so. Dik, his adolescent brashness beaten down by terror, nevertheless regarded Burl's stained weapon with the inevitable envy of the half-grown for achievement. He saw something half-buried in the soil and—after a fearful glance behind—he moved aside to tug at it. It was part of the armour of a former rhinoceros beetle. Tet joined him. They made an act of great daring of lingering to find themselves weapons as near as possible to Burl's.

A quarter-mile on, the fugitives passed a struggling milkweed plant, no more than twenty feet high and already scabrous with scale and rusts upon its lower parts. Ants marched up and down its stalk in a steady single file, placing aphids from their nearby ant-city on suitable spots to feed—and to multiply as only parthenogenic aphids can do. But already, on the far side of the milkweed, an ant-lion climbed up to do murder among them. The ant-lion, of course, was the larval form of a lace-wing fly. The aphids were its predestined prey.

Burl continued to march, holding Saya's hand. The reek of formic acid came to his nostrils. He ignored it. Ants were as much prey to his tribesmen, now, as crabs and crayfish to other, shore-dwelling tribesmen on long-forgotten Earth. But Burl was not concerned with food, now. He stalked on toward the mountain-slopes.

Dik and Tet brandished their new weapons. They

looked fearfully behind them. The monster from whom they
fled was lost in its gruesome feasting,—and they were a long
way from it, now. There was a steady, single-file procession
of ants, with occasional gaps in the line. The procession
passed the line through one of those gaps.

Beyond it, Tet and Dik conferred. They dared each
other. They went scrambling back to the line of ants. Their
weapons smote. The slaughtered ants died instantly and
were quickly dragged from the formic-acid-scented path.
The remaining ants went placidly on their way. The weapons struck again.

The two adolescents had to outdo each other. But they
had as much food as they could carry. Gloating—each
claiming to have been most daring and to have the largest
bag of game—they ran panting after the tribe. They grandly
distributed their take of game. It was a form of boasting. But
the tribesfolk accepted the gifts automatically. It was, after
all, food.

The two gangling boys, jabbering at each other, raced
back once more. Again they returned with dangling masses
of foodstuff—half-scores of foot-long creatures whose limbs,
at least, contained firm meat.

Behind, the ant-lion made his onslaught into the stu-
pidly feasting aphids, and warrior-ants took alarm and thrust
forward to offer battle. Tumult arose upon the milkweed.

But Burl led his followers toward the mountainside. He
reached a minor eminence and looked about him. Caution
was the price of existence on this world.

Two hundred feet away, a small scurrying horror raged
and searched among the rough-edged layers of what on
other worlds was called paper-mould or rock-tripe. Here it

was thick as quilting, and infinitesimal creatures denned under it. The sixteen-inch spider devoured them, making gluttonous sounds. But it was busy, and all spiders are relatively short-sighted.

Burl turned to Saya, and realized that all his tribe had followed him fearfully even to this small height he'd climbed only to look around from. Dor had taken advantage of Burl's pause. There was an empty cricket-shell partly overwhelmed by the fungoid soil. He tore free a now-hollow, sickle-shaped jaw. It was curved and sharp and deadly if properly wielded. Dor had seen Burl kill things. He had even helped. Now, very grimly, he tried to imagine killing something all alone. Jak saw him working on the sickle-shaped weapon. He tugged at the cricket's ransacked carcass for another weapon. Dik and Tet vaingloriously pretended to fight between themselves with their recently acquired instruments for killing. Jon wheezed and panted. Old Tama complained to herself in whispers, not daring to make sounds in the daylight. The rest waited until Burl should lead them further.

When Burl turned angry eyes upon them—he was beginning to do such things deliberately, now—they all regarded him humbly. Now they remembered that they had been hungry and he had gotten food for them, and they had been paralyzed by terror, and he dared to move. They definitely had a feeling of dependence upon him, for the present moment only. Later, their feeling of humbleness would diminish. In proportion as he met their needs for leadership, they would tend to try to become independent of him. His leadership would be successful in proportion as he taught them to lead themselves. But Burl perceived this only dimly.

At the moment it was pleasing to have all his tribe regard
him so worshipfully, even if not in quite the same fashion as
Saya. He was suddenly aware that now—at any rate while
they were so frightened—they would obey him. So he invented an order for them to obey.

"I carry sharp things," he said sternly. "Some of you
have gotten sharp things. Now everybody must carry sharp
things, to fight with."

Humbly, they scattered to obey. Saya would have gone
with them, but Burl held her back. He did not quite know
why. It could have been that the absoltue equality of the
sexes in cravenness was due to end, and for his own vanity
Burl would undertake the defense of Saya. He did not ana-
lyze so far. He did not want her to leave him, so he pre-
vented it.

The tribesfolk scattered. Dor went with his wife, to help
her arm herself. Jak uneasily followed his. Jon went timorously where the picked-over remnant of the cricket's
carcass might still yield an instrument of defense. Cori laid
her youngest child at Burl's feet while she went fearfully to
find some toothed instrument meeting Burl's specification
of sharpness.

There was a stifled scream. A ten-year-old boy—he was
Dik's younger brother—stood paralyzed. He stared in an
agony of horror at something that had stepped from behind
a misshapen fungoid object fifty yards from Burl, but less
than ten yards from him.

It was a pallidly greenish creature with a small head and
enormous eyes. It stood upright, like a man,—and it was a
few inches taller than a man. Its abdomen swelled gracefully
into a leaflike form. The boy faced it, paralyzed by horror,

and it stood stockstill. Its great, hideously spined arms were spread out in a pose of hypocritical benediction.

It was a partly grown praying mantis, not too long hatched. It stood rigid, waiting benignly for the boy to come closer or try to flee. If he fled, it would fling itself after him with a ferocity beside which the fury of a tiger would be kittenish. If he approached, its fanged arms would flash down, pierce his body, and hold him terribly fast by the needle-sharp hooks that were so much worse than trap-claws. And of course it would not wait for him to die before it began its meal.

All the small party of humans stood frozen. It may be questioned whether they were filled with horror for the boy, or cast into a deeper abyss of despair by the sight of a half-grown mantis. Only Burl, so far, had any notion of actually leaving the valley. To the rest, the discovery of one partly mature praying mantis meant that there would be hundreds of others. It would be impossible to evade the tiny, slavering demons which were the brood of the great spider. It would be impossibility multiplied to live where a horde of small— yet vastly larger—fiends lived, raising their arms in a semblance of blessing before they did murder.

Only Burl was capable of thought, and this was because vanity filled him. He had commanded and had been obeyed. Now obedience was forgotten because there was this young mantis. If the men had dreamed of fighting it, it could have destroyed any number of them by sheer ferocity and its arsenal of knives and daggers. But Burl was at once furious and experienced. He had encountered such a middle-sized monster, when alone, and deliberately had experimented with it. In consequence he could dare to rage. He ran toward the mantis. He swung the small corpse of an ant—killed by Tet only minutes since—and hurled it past the terror-fascinated boy. He had hurled it at the mantis.

It struck. And insects simply do not think. Something hurtled at the ghastly young creature. Its arms struck ferociously to defend itself. The ant was heavy. Poised upright in its spectral attitude, the mantis was literally flung backward. But it rolled over, fighting the dead ant with that frenzy which is not so much ferocity as mania.

The small boy fled, hysterically, once the insect's attention was diverted.

The human tribe gathered around Burl many hundreds of yards away—again uphill. He was their rendezvous because of the example set by Cori. She had left her baby with Burl. When Burl dashed from the spot, Saya had quite automatically followed the instinct of any female for the young of its kind. She'd snatched up the baby before she fled. And—of course—she'd joined Burl when the immediate danger was over.

The floor of the valley seemed a trifle indistinct, from here. The mist that hung always in the air partly veiled the details of its horrors. It was less actual, not quite as deadly as it once had seemed.

Burl said fiercely to his followers:

"Where are the sharp things?"

The tribesfolk looked at one another, numbly. Then Jon muttered rebelliously, and old Tama raised her voice in shrill complaint. Burl had led them to this! There had been only the red dust in the place from which they had come, but here was a hunting-spider and its young and also a new hatching of mantises! They could dodge the red dust, but how could they escape the deaths that waited them here?

Ai! Ai! Burl had persuaded them to leave their home and brought them here to die. . . .

Burl glared about him. It was neither courage nor resolution, but he had come to realize that to be admired by one's fellows was a splendid sensation. The more one was admired, the better. He was enraged that anyone dared to despair instead of thinking admiringly about his remarkableness.

"I," said Burl haughtily, "am not going to stay here. I go to a place where there are neither spiders nor mantises. Come!"

He held out his hand to Saya. She gave the child to Cori and confidently moved to follow him. Burl stalked grandly away and she went with him. He went uphill. Naturally! There were spiders and mantises in the valley—so many that to stay there meant death. So he moved to go somewhere else.

And this was the climactic event that changed the whole history of humanity upon the forgotten planet. Up to this point, there may have been other individuals who had accomplished somewhat of Burl's kind of leadership. A few may have learned courage. It is possible that some even led their tribesfolk upon migrations in search of safer lands to live in. But until Burl led his people out of a valley filled with food, up a mountainside toward the unknown, it was simply impossible for humans to rise permanently above the status of hunted vermin; at the mercy of monstrous mindless creatures; whose forbears had most ironically been brought to this planet to prepare it for humans to live on.

Burl was the first man to lead his fellows toward the heights.

There Is Such a Thing as Sunshine!

9

THE SUN THAT shone upon the forgotten planet was actually very near. It shone on the top of the cloud-bank, and the clouds glowed with dazzling whiteness. It shone on the mountain-peaks where they penetrated the mist, and the peaks were warmed, and there was no snow anywhere despite the height. There were winds, here where the sun yielded sensible heat. The sky was very blue. At the edge of the plateau—from which the cloud-banks were down instead of up—the mountainsides seemed to descend into a sea of milk. Great undulations in the mist had the semblance of waves, which moved with great deliberation toward the shores. They seemed sometimes to break in slow-motion against the mountain-walls where they were cliff-like, and sometimes they seemed to flow up gentler inclinations like water flowing up a beach. But all of this was very deliberate indeed, because the cloud-waves were sometimes twenty miles from crest to crest.

The look of things was different on the highlands. This

part of the unnamed world, no less than the lowlands, had
been seeded with life on two separate occasions. Once the
seeding was with bacteria and moulds and lichens to break
up the rocks and make soil of them, and once with seeds and
insect-eggs and such living things as might sustain themselves immediately they were hatched. But here on the
highlands the different climatic conditions had allowed
other seedlings and creatures to survive together.

Here moulds and yeasts and rusts were stunted by the
sunlight. Grasses and weeds and trees survived, instead.
This was an ideal environment for plants that needed sunlight to form chlorophyl, with which to make use of the soil
that had been formed. So on the highlands the vegetation
was almost earthlike. And there was a remarkable side-effect
on the fauna which had been introduced in the same manner and at the same time as the creatures down below. In
coolness which amounted to a temperate climate, there developed no such frenzy of life as made the nightmare jungles
under the clouds. Plants grow at a slower rate than fungi,
and less luxuriantly. There was no vast supply of food for
large-sized plant eaters. Insects which were to survive, here,
could not grow to be monsters. Moreover, the nights here
were chill. Very many insects grow torpid in the cool of a
temperate-zone night, but warm up to activity soon after
sunrise. But a large creature, made torpid by cold, will not
revive so quickly. If large enough, it will not become fully
active until close to dark. On the plateau, the lowland monsters would starve in any case. But more—they would have
only a fraction of each day of full activity.

So there was a necessary limit to the size of the creatures that lived above the clouds. To humans from other

planets, the life on the plateau would not have seemed horrifying at all. Save for the absence of birds to sing, and a lack of small mammals to hunt or merely to enjoy, the untouched, sunlit plateau with its warm days and briskly chill nights would have impressed most civilized men as an ideal habitation.

But Burl and his followers were hardly prepared to see it that way at first glance. If told about it in advance, they would have thought of it with despair.

But they did not know beforehand. They toiled upward, their leader moved by such ridiculous motives of pride and vanity as have caused men to achieve greatness throughout all history. Two great continents were discovered back on Earth by a man trying to get spices to hide the gamey flavor of half-spoiled meat, and the power that drives mile-long space-craft was first discovered and tamed by men making bombs to destroy their fellows. There were precedents for foolish motives producing results far from foolishness.

The trudging, climbing folk crawled up the hillside. They reached a place high above the valley Burl had led them to. That valley grew misty in appearance. Presently it could no longer be seen at all. The mist they had taken for granted, all their lives, hid from them everything but the slanting stony wall up which they climbed. The stone was mostly covered by bluish-green rock-tripe in partly overlapping sheets. Such stuff is always close behind the bacteria which first attack a rock-face. On a slope, it clings while soil is washed downward as fast as it is formed. The people never ate rock-tripe, of course. It produces frightening cramps. In time they might learn that when thoroughly dried it can be cooked to pliability again and eaten with some satisfaction. But so far they neither knew dryness nor fire.

Nor had they ever known such surroundings as presently enveloped them. As slanting rocky mountainside, which stretched up frighteningly to the very sky. Grayness overhead. Grayness also to one side—the side away from the mountain. And equal grayness below. The valley from which they had come could no longer be seen even as a different shading of the mist. And as they scrambled and trudged after Burl, his followers gradually became aware of the utter strangeness of all about them. For one result, they grew sick and dizzy. To them it seemed that all solidity was slowly tilting. Had they been superstitious, they might have thought of demons preparing to punish them for daring to come to such a place. But—quaintly enough—Burl's followers had developed no demonology. Your typical savage is resolved not to think, but he does have leisure to want. He makes gods and devils out of his nightmares, and gambles on his own speculations to the extent of offering blackmail to demons if they will only let him alone or—preferably— give him more of the things he wants.

But the superstitions of savages involve the payment of blackmail in exact proportion to their prosperity. The Eskimos of Earth lived always on the brink of starvation. They could not afford the luxury of tabus and totem animals whose flesh must not be eaten, and forbidden areas which might contain food.

Religion there was, among Burl's people, but superstition was not. No humans, anywhere, can live without religion, but on Earth Eskimos did with a minimum of superstitions—they could afford no more—and the humans of the forgotten planet could not afford any at all.

Therefore they climbed desperately despite the unparalleled state of things about them. There was no horizon,
but they had never seen a horizon. Their feeling was that
what had been "down" was now partly "behind" and they
feared lest a toppling universe ultimately let them fall toward that grayness they considered the sky.

But all kept on. To lag behind would be to be abandoned in this place where all known sensations were turned
topsy-turvy. None of them could imagine turning back.
Even old Tama, whimpering in a whisper as she struggled to
keep up, merely complained bitterly of her fate. She did not
even think of revolt. If Burl had stopped, all his followers
would have squatted down miserably to wait for death.
They had no thought of adventure or any hope of safety.
The only goodnesses they could imagine were food and the
nearness of other humans. They had food—nobody had
abandoned any of the dangling ant-bodies Tet and Dik had
distributed before the climb began. They would not be separated from their fellows.

Burl's motivation was hardly more distinct. He had
started uphill in a judicious mixture of fear and injured vanity and desperation. There was nothing to be gained by
going back. The terrors at hand were no greater than those
behind, so there was no reason not to go ahead.

They came to a place where the mountain-flank sank
inward. There was a flat space, and behind it a winding
cañon of sorts like a vast crack in the mountain's substance.
Burl breasted the curving edge and found flatness beyond it.
He stopped short.

The mouth of the cañon was perhaps fifty yards from
the lip of the downward slope. So much space was practically level, and on it were toadstools and milkweed—two of

them—and there was food. It was a small, isolated asylum
for life such as they were used to. They could—it was possible that they could—have found a place of safety here.

But the possibility was not the fact. They saw the spider-web at once. It was slung between the opposite cañon-
walls by cables all of two hundred feet long. The radiating
cables reached down to anchorages on stone. The snare-
threads, winding out and out in that logarithmic spiral
whose properties men were so astonished to discover, were
fully a yard apart. The web was for giant game. It was empty
now, but Burl saw the telegraph-cord which ran from the
very center of the web to the web-maker's lurking-place.
There was a rocky shelf on the cañon-wall. On it rested the
spider, almost invisible against the stone, with one furry leg
touching the cable. The slightest touch on any part of the
web would warn it instantly.

Burl's followers accumulated behind him. Old Jon's
wheezing was audible. Tama ceased her complaints to survey this spot. It might be—it could be—a haven, and she
would have to find new and different things to complain
about in consequence. The spider-web itself, of course, was
no reason for them to be alarmed. Web-spiders do not hunt.
Their males do, but they are rarely in the neighborhood of a
web save at mating-time. The web itself was no reason not
to settle here. But there was a reason.

The ground before the web—between the web and
themselves—was a charnel-house of murdered creatures.
Half-inch-thick wing-cases of dead beetles and the cleaned-
out carapaces of other giants. The ovipositor of an ichneu-
mon-fly—six feet of springy, slender, deadly-pointed tube—
and the abdomen-plates of bees and the draggled antennae
of moths and butterflies.

Something very terrible lived in this small place. The mountainsides were barren of food for big flying things. Anything which did fly this high for any reason would never land on sloping foodless stone. It would land here. And very obviously it would die. Because something—Something— killed things as they came. It denned back in the cañon where they could not see it. It dined here.

The humans looked and shivered, all but Burl. He cast his eyes about for better weapons than he possessed. He chose for himself a magnificent lance grown by some dead thing for its own defense. He pulled it out of the ground.

It was utterly silent, here on the heights. No sounds from the valley rose so high. There was no noise except the small creakings made as Burl strove to free the new, splendid weapon for himself.

That was why he heard the gasp which somebody uttered in default of a scream that would not be uttered. It was choked, a strangled, an inarticulate sobbing noise.

He saw its cause.

There was a thing moving toward the folk from the recesses of the cañon. It moved very swiftly. It moved upon stiltlike, impossibly attenuated legs of impossible length and inconceivable number. Its body was the thickness of Burl's own. And from it came a smell of such monstrous foetor that any man, smelling it, would gag and flee even without fear to urge him on. The creature was a monstrous millipede, forty feet in length, with features of purest, unadulterated horror.

It did not appear to plan to spring. Its speed of movement did not increase as it neared the tribesfolk. It was not rushing, like the furious charge of the murderers Burl's tribe knew. It simply flowed sinuously toward them with no appearance of haste, but at a rate of speed they could not conceivably outrun.

At sixty yards, Burl shouted hoarsely. As the thing flowed under the cables of the spider's web, he was swinging a small black glistening missile. He flung it.

Sticklike legs twitched upward and caught the spinning body of an ant. The creature stopped, and turned its head about and seized the object its side-legs had grasped. It devoured it. Burl shouted again and again.

There was a rain of missiles upon the creature. But they were not to hurt it, but to divert its incredibly automaton-like attention. Its legs seized the things flung to it. It was not possible to miss. Ten, fifteen—twenty of the items of small-game were grasped in mid-air, as if they were creatures in flight.

Burl's shoutings took effect. His people fled to the side of the level lip of ground. They climbed frantically past the opening of the valley. They fled toward the heights.

Burl was the last to retreat. The monstrous millipede stood immobile, trapped for the moment by the gratification of all its desires. It was absorbed by the multitude of tiny tidbits with which it had been provided.

It was a fact to Burl's honor that he debated a frantic attack upon the monster in its insane absorption. But the strangling stench was deterrent enough. He fled—the last of his band of fugitives to leave the place where the monstrous creature lived and preyed. As he left it, it was still crunching the small meals, one by one, with which the folk had supplied it.

They went on up the mountain-flank. It was not to be supposed, of course, that the creature could not move about the slanting rock-surface. Unquestionably it roamed far and wide, upon occasion, But its own foetid reek would make impossible any idea of trailing the humans by scent. And, climbing desperately as the humans did, it would be unable to see them when they were past the first protuberance of the mountain.

In twenty minutes they slackened their pace. Exhaustion prompted it. Caution ordered it. Because here they saw another small island of flatness in the slanting universe which was all they could see save mist. It was simply a place where boulders had piled up, and soil had formed, and there was a miniature haven for life other than moulds which could grow on naked stone.

Actually, there was a space a hundred feet by fifty on which wholly familiar mushrooms grew. It was a thicket like a detached section of the valley itself. Well-known edible fungi grew here. They were gray puffballs. And from it came the cheerful loud chirping of some small beetle, arrived at this spot nobody could possibly know how, but happily ensconced in a separate bit of mushroom-jungle remote from the dangers of the valley. If it was small enough, it would even be safe from the reeking horror of the cañon just below it.

They broke off edible mushrooms here and ate. And this could have been safety for them—save for the giant millipede no more than half a mile below. Old Jon wheezed querulously that here was food and there was no need for them to go further, just now. Here was food. . . .

Burl regarded him with knitted brows. Jon's reaction was natural enough. The tribesfolk had never tended to think for the future because it was impossible to make use of

such planning. Even Burl could easily enough have accepted
the fact that this was safety for the moment and food for the
moment. But it happened that to settle down here until
driven out would—and at this moment—have deprived him
of the authority he had so recently learned to enjoy.

"You stay," he with haughtily, to Jon. "I go on, to a
better place where nothing is to be feared at all!"

He held out his hand to Saya. He assailed the slope
again, heading upward in the mist.

His tribe followed him. Dik and Tet, of course, because
they were boys and Burl led on to high adventures in which
so far nobody had been killed. Dor followed because—he
being the strongest man in the tribe—he had thoughtfully
realized that his strength was not as useful as Burl's brains
and other qualities. Cori followed because she had children,
and they were safer where Burl led than anywhere else. The
others followed to avoid being left alone.

The procession toiled on and up. Presently Burl noticed
that the air seemed clearer, here. It was not the misty, only
half transparent stuff of the valley. He could see for miles to
right and left. He realized the curvature of the mountain-
face. But he could not see the valley. The mist hid that.

Suddenly he realized that he saw the cloudbank overhead as an object. He had never thought of it specifically
before. To him it had been simply the sky. Now he saw an
indefinite lower surface which yet definitely hid the heights
toward which he moved. He and his followers were less than
a thousand feet below it. It appeared to Burl that presently
he would run into an obstacle which would simply keep him
from going any further. The idea was disheartening. But
until it happened he obstinately climbed on.

He observed that the thing which was the sky did not stay still. It moved, though slowly. A little higher, he could see that there were parts of it which were actually lower than he was. They moved also, but they moved away from him as often as they moved toward him. He had no experience of any dangerous things which did not leap at its victims. Therefore he was not afraid.

In fact, presently he noticed that the whiteness which was the cloud-layer seemed to retreat before him. He was pleased. Weak things like humans fled from enemies. Here was something which fled at his approach! His followers undoubtedly saw the same thing! Burl had killed spiders. He was a remarkable person. This unknown white stuff was afraid of him. Therefore it was wise to stay close to Burl. Burl found his vanity inflamed by the fact that always— even at its thickest—the white cloud-stuff never came nearer than some dozens of feet. He swaggered as he led his people up.

And presently there was brightness about them. It was a greater brightness than the tribesfolk had ever known. They knew daylight as a grayness in which one could see. Here was brightness that shone. They were not accustomed to brightness.

They were not accustomed to silence, either. The noises of the valley were like all the noises of the lowlands. They had been in the ears of every one of the human beings since they could hear at all. They had gradually diminished as the valley dropped behind them. Now, in the radiant white mist which was the cloud-layer, there were no sounds at all, and the fact was suddenly startling.

They blinked in the brightness. When they spoke to

each other, they spoke in whispers. The stone underfoot was not even lichen-covered, here. It was bare and bright and glistened with wetness. The light they experienced took on a golden tint. All of these things were utterly unparalleled, but the stillness was a hush instead of a menacing silence. The golden light could not possibly be associated with fear. The people of the forgotten planet felt, most likely, the sort of promise in this shining tranquility which before they had known only in dreams. But this was no dream.

They came up through the surface of a sea of mist, and they saw before them a shore of sunshine. They saw blue sky and sunlight for the first time. The light smote their shins and brilliantly colored furry garments. It glittered in changing, ever-more-colorful flashes upon cloaks made of butterfly wings. It sparkled on the great lance carried by Burl in the lead, and the quite preposterous weapons borne by his followers.

The little party of twenty humans waded ashore through the last of the thinning white stuff which was cloud. They gazed about them with wondering, astonished eyes. The sky was blue. There was green grass. And again there was sound. It was the sound of wind blowing among trees, and of things living in the sunshine.

They heard insects, but they did not know what they heard. The shrill small musical whirrings; the high-pitched small cries which made an elfin melody everywhere—these were totally strange. All things were new to their eyes, and an enormous exultation filled them. From deep-buried ancestral memories they somehow knew that what they saw was right, was normal, was appropriate and proper, and that this was the kind of world in which humans belonged, rather than the seething horror of the lowlands. They breathed clean air for the first time in many generations.

Burl shouted in his triumph, and his voice echoed among trees and hillsides.

It was time for the plateau to ring with the shouting of a man in triumph!

Men Climb Up to Savagery

10

T HEY HAD FOOD for days. They had brought mushroom from the isolated thicket not too far beneath the clouds. There were the ants that Dik and Tet had distributed grandly, and not all of which had been used to secure escape from the cañon of the millipede. Had they found other food immediately, they would have settled down comfortably in the fashion normal to creatures whose idea of bliss is a secure hiding-place and food on hand so they do not have to leave it. Somehow they believed that this high place of bright light and new colors was secure. But they had no hiding-place. And though they did accept with the unreasoning faith of children and savages that there were no enemies here, they still wanted one.

They found a cave. It was small, so that it would be crowded with all of them in it, but as it turned out, this was fortunate. At some time it had been occupied by some other creature, but the dirt which floored it had settled flat and showed no tracks. It retained faint traces of a smell which was unfamiliar but not unpleasing—it held no connotation of danger. Ants stank of formic acid plus the musky odor of their particular city. One could identify not only the kind of ant, but its home city, by sniffing at an ant-trail. Spiders had their own hair-raising odor. The smell of a praying-mantis was acrid, and all beetles reeked of decay. And of course there were those bugs whose main defense was an effluvium which tended to strangle all but the smell's happy possessor. This faint smell in the cave was different. The humans thought vaguely that it might possibly be another kind of man.

Actually, it was the smell of a warm-blooded animal. But Burl and his fellows knew of no warm-blooded creature but themselves.

They had come above the clouds a bare two hours before sunset—of which they knew nothing. For an hour they marveled, staying close together. They were especially astounded by the sun, since they could not bear to look at it. But presently, being savages, they accepted it matter-of-factly.

They could not cease to wonder at the vegetation about them. They were accustomed only to gigantic fungi and the few straggling plants which tried so desperately to bear seed before they were devoured. Here they saw many plants and no fungi—and they did not see anything they recognized as insects. They looked only for large things.

They were astounded by the slenderness and toughness of the plants. Grass fascinated them, and weeds. A large part of their courage came from the absence of debris upon the ground. The hunting-grounds of spiders were marked by grisly remnants of finished meals, and where mantises roamed there were bits of transparent beetle-wings and sharp spiny bits of armor not tasty enough to be consumed. Here, in the first hour of their exploration, they saw no sign that an insect like the lowland ones had ever been in this place at all. But they could not believe the monsters never came. They correctly—and pessimistically—assumed that their coming was only rare.

The cave was a great relief. Trees did not grow close enough to give them a feeling of safety—though they were ludicrously amazed at the invincible hardness of tree trunks. They had never known anything but insect-armor and stone which was as hard as the trunks of those growing things. They found nothing to eat, but they were not yet hungry. They did not worry about food while they still had remnants from their climb.

When the sun sank low and crimson colorings filled the west, they were less happy. They watched the glory of their first sunset with scared, incredulous eyes. Yellows and reds and purples reared toward the zenith. It became possible to look at the sun directly. They saw it descend behind something they could not guess at. Then there was darkness.

The fact stunned them. So night came like this!

Then they saw the stars for the first time, as they came singly into being. And the folk from the lowland crowded frantically into the cave with its faint odor of having once been occupied by something else. They filled the cave tightly. But Burl had some reluctance to admit his terror. He and Saya were the last to enter.

And nothing happened. Nothing. The sounds of sunset continued. They were strange but soothing and somehow—

again ancestral memory spoke comfortingly—they were the way night-sounds ought to be. Burl and the others could not possibly know it, but for the first time in forty generations on the forgotten planet, human beings were in an environment really suited to them. It had a rightness and a goodness which was obvious in spite of its novelty. And because of Burl's own special experiences, he was a little bit better able to estimate novelties than the rest.

He listened to the night-noises from close by the cave's small entrance. He heard the breathing of his tribesfolk. He felt the heat of their bodies, keeping the crowded enclosure warm enough for all. Saya held fast to his hand, for the reassurance of the contact. He was wakeful, and thinking very busily and painfully, but Saya was not thinking at all. She was simply proud of Burl.

She felt, to be sure, a tumult which was fear of the unknown and relief from much greater fear of the familiar. She felt warm, prideful memories of the sight of Burl leading and commanding the others. She had absorbing fresh memories of the look and feel of sunshine, and mental pictures of sky and grass and tress which she had never seen before. Confusedly she remembered that Burl had killed a spider, no less, and he had shown how to escape a praying-mantis by flinging it an ant, and he had grandly led the others up a mountainside it had never occurred to anybody else to climb. And the giant millipede would have devoured them all, but that Burl gave commands and set the example, and he had marched magnificently up the mountainside when it seemed that all the cosmos twisted and prepared to drop them into an inverted sky. . . .

Saya dozed. And Burl sat awake, listening, and presently with fast-beating heart he slipped out of the entrance to the cave and stared about him in the night.

There was coolness such as he had never known before, but night-fall was not long past. There were smells in the air he had never before experienced—green things growing, and the peculiar odor of wind that has been bathed in sunshine, and the oddly satisfying smell of resinous trees.

But Burl raised his eyes to the heavens. He saw the stars in all their glory, and he was the first human in two thousand years and more to look at them from this planet. There were myriads upon myriads of them, varying in brightness from stabbing lights to infinitesimal twinklings. They were of every possible color. They hung in the sky above him, immobile and unthreatening. They had not descended. They were very beautiful.

Burl stared. And then he noticed that he was breathing deeply, with a new zest. He was filling his lungs with clean, cool, fragrant air such as men were intended to beathe from the beginning, and of which Burl and many others had been deprived. It was almost intoxicating to feel so splendidly alive and unafraid.

There was a slight sound. Saya stood beside him, trembling a little. To leave the others had required great courage, but she had come to realize that if Burl was in danger she wished to share it.

They heard the nightwind and the orchestra of nightsingers. They wandered aside from the cave-mouth and Saya found completely primitive and satisfying pride in the courage of Burl, who was actually not afraid of the dark! Her own uneasiness became something which merely added savor to her pride in him. She followed him wherever he went, to examine this and consider that in the nighttime. It gave her enormous satisfaction at once to think of danger and to feel so safe because of his nearness.

Presently they head a new sound in the night. It was very far away, and not in the least like any sound they had ever heard before. It changed in pitch as insect-cries do not. It was a baying, yelping sound. It rose, and held the higher note, and abruptly dropped in pitch before it ceased. Minutes later it came again.

Saya shivered, but Burl said thoughtfully:

"That is a good sound."

He didn't know why. Saya shivered again. She said reluctantly:

"I am cold."

It had been a rare sensation in the lowlands. It came only after one of the infrequent thunderstorms, when wetted human bodies were exposed to the gusty winds that otherwise never blew. But here the nights grew cold after sundown. The heat of the ground would radiate to outer space with no clouds to intercept it, and before dawn the temperature might drop nearly to freezing. On a planet so close to the sun, however, there would hardly be more than light hoar-frost at any time.

The two of them went back to the cave. It was warm there, because of the close packing of bodies and many breaths. Burl and Saya found places to rest and dozed off, Saya's hand again trustfully in Burl's.

He still remained awake for a long time. He thought of the stars, but they were too strange to estimate. He thought of the trees and grass. But most of his impressions of this upper world were so remote from previous knowledge that he could only accept them as they were and defer reflecting upon them until later. He did feel an enormous complacency at having led his followers here, though.

But the last thing he actually thought about, before his eyes blinked shut in sleep, was that distant howling noise he had heard in the night. It was totally novel in kind, and yet there was something buried among the items of his racial heritage that told him it was good.

He was first awake of all the tribesmen and he looked out into the cold and pallied grayness of before-dawn. He saw trees. One side was brightly lighted by comparison, and the other side was dark. He heard the tiny singing noises of the inhabitants of this place. Presently he crawled out of the cave again.

The air was biting in its chill. It was an excellent reason why the giant insects could not live here, but it was invigorating to Burl as he breathed it in. Presently he looked curiously for the source of the peculiar one-sided light.

He saw the top of the sun as it peered above the eastern cloud-bank. The sky grew lighter. He blinked and saw it rise more fully into view. He thought to look upward, and the stars that had bewildered him were nearly gone.

He ran to call Saya.

The rest of the tribe waked as he roused her. One by one they followed to watch their first sunrise. The men gaped at the sun as it filled the east with colorings, and rose and rose above the seemingly steaming layer of clouds, and then appeared to spring free of the horizon and swim on upward.

The women stared with all their eyes. The children blinked, and shivered, and crept to their mothers for warmth. The women enclosed them in their cloaks, and they thawed and peered out once more at the glory of sunshine and the day. Very soon, too, they realized that warmth came from the great shining body in the sky. The children presently discovered a game. It was the first game they had ever played. It consisted of running into a shaded place until they shivered, and then of running out into warm sunshine once more. Until this dawning, fear was the motive for such playing as they did. Now they gleefully made a game of sunshine.

In this first morning of their life above the clouds, the tribesmen ate of the food they had brought from below. But there was not an indefinite amount of food left. Burl ate, and considered darkly, and presently summoned his followers' attention. They were quite contented and for the moment felt no need for his guidance. But he felt need of admiration.

He spoke abruptly:

"We do not want to go back to the place we came from," he said sternly. "We must look for food here, so we can stay for always. Today we find food."

It was a seizure of the initiative. It was the linking of what the folk most craved with obedience to Burl. It was the device by which dictators seize power, and it was the instinctive action of a leader.

The eating men murmured agreement. There was a certain definite idea of goodness—not virtue, but of things desirable—associated with what Burl did and what he commanded. His tribe was gradually forming a habit of obedience, though it was a very fragile habit up to now.

He led them exploring as soon as they had eaten. All of

them, of course. They straggled irregularly behind him. They came to a brook and regarded it with amazement. There were no leeches. No greenish algae. No foaming masses of scum. It was clear! Greatly daring, Burl tasted it. He drank the first really potable water in a very long time for his race on this planet. It was not fouled by drainage through moulds or rusts.

Dor drank after him. Jak. Cori tasted, and instantly bade her children drink. Even old Tama drank suspiciously, and then raised her voice in shrill complaint that Burl had not led them to this place sooner. Tet and Dik became convinced that there were no deadly things lurking in it, and splashed each other. Dik slipped and sat down hard on white stuff that yielded and almost splashed. He got up and looked fearfully at what he thought might be a deadly slime. Then he yelped shrilly.

He had sat down on and crushed part of a bed of mushrooms. But they were tiny, clean, and appetizing. They were miniatures of the edible mushrooms the tribe fed on.

Burl smelled and finally tasted one. It was, of course, nothing more or less than a perfectly normal edible mushroom, growing to the size that mushrooms originally grew on Earth. It grew on a shaded place in enormously rich soil. It had been protected from direct sunlight by trees, but it had not had the means or the stimulus to become a monster.

Burl ate it. He carefully composed his features. Then he announced the find to his followers. There was food here, he told them sternly, but in this splendid world to which he had led them, food was small. There would be no great enemies here, but the food would have to be sought in small

objects instead of great ones. They must look at this place
and seek others like it, in order to find food. . . .

The tribesmen were doubtful. But they plucked mushrooms—whole ones!—instead of merely breaking off parts
of their tops. With deep astonishment they recognized the
miniature objects as familiar things ensmalled. These mushrooms had the same savor, but they were not coarse or
stringy or tough like the giants. They melted in the mouth!
Life in this place to which Burl had led them was delectable! Truly the doings of Burl were astonishing!

When the oldest of Cori's children found a beetle on a
leaf, and they recognized it, and instead of being bigger than
a man and a thing to flee from, it was less than an inch in
size and helpless against them—they were entranced. From
that moment onward they would really follow Burl anywhere, in the happy conviction that he could only bring
good to everybody.

The opinion could have drawbacks, and it need not be
always even true, but Burl did nothing to discourage it.

And then, near midday, they made a discovery even
greater than that of familiar food in unfamiliar sizes. They
were struggling, at the time, through a vast patch of bushes
with thorns on them—they were not used to thorns—which
they deeply distrusted. Eventually they would find out that
the glistening dark fruit were blackberries, and would rejoice
in them, but at this first encounter they were uneasy. In the
midst of such an untouched berry-patch they heard noises in
the distance.

The sound was made up of cries of varying pitch, some
of which were loud and abrupt, and others longer and less
loud. The people did not understand them in the least.

They could have been cries of human beings, perhaps, but they were not cries of pain. Also they were not language. They seemed to express a tremendous, zestful excitement. They had no overtone of horror. And Burl and his folk had known of no excitement among insects except frenzy. They could not imagine what sort of tumult this could be.

But to Burl these sounds had something of the timbre of the yelping noises of the night before. He had felt drawn to that sound. He liked it. He liked this.

He led the way boldly toward the agitated noises. Presently—after half a mile or so—he and his people came out of breast-high weeds. Saya was immediately behind him. The others trailed—Tama complaining bitterly that there was no need to track down sounds which could only mean danger. They emerged in a space of bare stone above a small and grassy amphitheatre. The tumult came from its center.

A pack of dogs was joyously attacking something that Burl could not see clearly. They were dogs. They barked zestfully, and they yelped and snarled and yapped in a dozen different voices, and they were having a thoroughly good time—though it might not be so good for the thing they attacked.

One of them sighted the humans. He stopped stock-still and barked. The others whirled and saw the humans as they came out into view. The tumult ceased abruptly.

There was silence. The tribesmen saw creatures with four legs only. They had never before seen any living thing with fewer than six—except men. Spiders had eight. The dogs did not have mandibles. They did not have wing-cases. They did not act like insects. It was stupefying!

And the dogs saw men, whom they had never seen

before. Much more important, they smelled men. And the difference between man-smell and insect-smell was so vast—because through hundreds of generations the dogs had not smelled anything with warm blood save their own kind—the difference in smell was so great in kind that the dogs did not react with suspicion, but with a fascinated curiosity. This was an unparalleled smell. It was, even in its novelty, an overwhelmingly satisfying smell.

The dogs regarded the men with their heads on one side, sniffing in the deepest possible amazement—amazement so intense that they could not possibly feel hostility. One of them whined a little because he did not understand.

PECULIARLY ENOUGH, IT was a matter of topography. The plateau which reached above the clouds rose with a steep slope from the valley from which a hunting-spider's brood had driven the men. This was on the eastern edge of the plateau. On the west, however, the highland was subject to an indentation which almost severed it. No more than twenty miles from where Burl's group had climbed to sunshine, there was a much more gradual slope downward. There, mushroom-forest grew almost to the cloud-layer. From there, giant insects strayed up and onto the plateau itself.

They could not live above the clouds, of course. There was not food enough for their insatiable hunger. Especially at night, it was too cold to allow them to stay active. But they did stray from their normal environment, and some of them did reach the sunshine, and perhaps some of them blundered back down to their mushroom-forests again. But those which did not stumble back were chilled to torpor during their first night underneath the stars. They were only partly active on the second day—if, indeed, they were active at all. Few or none recovered from their second night's coldness. None at all kept their full ferocity and deadliness.

And this was how the dogs survived. They were certainly descended from dogs on the wrecked space-ship—the *Icarus*—whose crew had landed on this planet some forty-odd human generations since. The humans of today had no memories of the ship, and the dogs surely had no traditions. But just because those early dogs surely had less intelligence, they had more useful instincts. Perhaps the first generations of castaways bred dogs in their first few desperate centuries, hoping that dogs could help them survive. But no human civilization could survive in the lowlands. The humans went back to the primitive state of their race and lived as furtive vermin among monsters. Dogs could not survive there, though humans did linger on, so somehow the dogs took to the heights. Perhaps dogs survived their masters. Perhaps some were abandoned or driven away. But dogs had reached the highlands. And they did survive because giant insects blundered up after them—and could not survive in a proper environment for dogs and men.

There was even reason for the dogs remaining limited in number, and keenly intelligent. The food-supply was limited. When there were too many dogs, their attacks on stumbling insect giants were more desperate and made earlier, before the monsters' ferocity was lessened. So more dogs died. Then there was an adjustment of the number of dogs to the food-supply. There was also a selection of those too intelligent to attack rashly. Yet those who had insufficient courage would not eat.

In short, the dogs who now regarded men with bright,

interested eyes were very sound dogs. They had the intelligence needed for survival. They did not attack anything im-
prudently, but they also knew that it was not necessary to be
more than reasonably wary of insects in general—not even
spiders unless they were very newly arrived from the steaming lowlands. So the dogs regarded men with very much the
same astonished interest with which the men regarded the
dogs.

Burl saw immediately that the dogs did not act with the
blind ferocity of insects, but with an interested, estimative
intelligence strikingly like that of men. Insects never examined anything. They fled or they fought. Those who were
not carnivorous had no interest in anything but food, and
those who were meat-eaters lumbered insanely into battle at
the bare sight of possible prey. The dogs did neither. They
sniffed and they considered.

Burl said sharply to his followers:

"Stay here!"

He walked slowly down into the amphitheatre. Saya
followed him instantly. Dogs moved warily aside. But they
raised their noses and sniffed. They were long, luxurious
sniffs. The smell of humankind was a good smell. Dogs had
lived hundreds of their generations without having it in their
nostrils, but before that there were thousands of generations
to whom that smell was a necessity.

Burl reached the object the dogs had been attacking. It
lay on the grass, throbbing painfully. It was the larva of an
azure-blue moth which spread ten-foot wings at nightfall.
The time for its metamorphosis was near, and it had traveled blindly in search of a place where it could spin its cocoon safely and change to its winged form. It had come to

another world—the world above the clouds. It could find no proper place. Its stores of fat had protected it somewhat from the chill. But the dogs had found it as it crawled blindly.

Burl considered. It was the custom of wasps to sting creatures like this at a certain special spot—apparently marked for them by a tuft of dark fur.

Burl thrust home with his lance. The point pierced that particular spot. The creature died quickly and without agony. The thought to kill was an inspiration. Then instinct followed. Burl cut off meat for his tribesmen. The dogs offered no objection. They were well-fed enough. Burl and Saya, together, carried the meat back to the other tribesfolk. On the way Burl passed within two yards of a dog which regarded him with extreme intentness and almost a wistful expression. Burl's smell did not mean game. It meant — something the dog struggled helplessly to remember. But it was good.

"I have killed the thing," said Burl to the dog, in the tone of one addressing an equal. "You can go and eat it now. I took only part of it."

The dog wagged its tail, and then backed away as if in confusion. After all, matters had not yet progressed to cordiality!

Burl and his people ate of what he had brought back. Many of the dogs—most of them—went to the feast Burl had left. Presently they were back. They had no reason to be hostile. They were fed. The humans offered them no injury, and the humans smelled of something that appealed to the deepest well-springs of canine nature.

Presently the dogs were close about the humans. They

were fascinated. And the humans were fascinated in return. Each of the people had a little of the feeling that Burl had experienced as the tribal leader. In the intent, absorbed and wholly unhostile regard of the dogs, even children felt flattered and friendly. And surely in a place where everything else was so novel and so satisfactory, it was possible to imagine friendliness with creatures which were not human, since assuredly they were not insects.

A similar state of mind existed among the dogs.

Saya had more meat than she desired. She glanced among the members of the tribe. All were supplied. She tossed it to a dog. He jerked away alertly, and then sniffed at it where it had dropped. A dog can always eat. He ate it.

"I wish you would talk to us," said Saya hopefully.

The dog wagged his tail.

"You do not look like us," said Saya interestedly, "but you act like we do. Not like the—Monsters."

The dog looked significantly at meat in Burl's hand. Burl tossed it. The dog caught it with a quick snap, swallowed it, wagged his tail briefly and came closer. It was a completely incredible action, but dogs and men were blood-kin on this planet. Besides, there was racial-memory rightness in friendship between men and dogs. It was not hindered by any past experience of either. They were the only warm-blooded creatures on this world. It was a kinship felt by both.

Presently Burl stood up and spoke politely to the dog. He addressed him with the same respect he would have given to another man. In all his life he had never felt equal to an insect, but he felt no arrogance toward this dog. He felt superior only to other men.

"We are going back to our cave," he said politely. "Maybe we will meet again."

He led his tribe back to the cave in which they spent the previous night. The dogs followed, ranging on either side. They were well-fed, with no memory of hostility to any creature which smelled of warm blood. They had an instinct without experience to dull it. The latter part of the journey back to the tribal cave was—if anybody had been qualified to notice it—remarkably like a group of dogs taking a walk with a group of people. It was companionable. It felt right.

That night Burl left the cave, as before, to look at the stars. This time Saya went with him matter-of-factly. But as they came out of the cave-entrance there was a stirring. A dog rose and stretched himself elaborately, yawning the while. When Burl and Saya moved away, he trotted amiably with them.

They talked to it, and the dog seemed pleased. It wagged its tail.

When morning came, the dogs were still waiting hopefully for the humans to come out. They appeared to expect the people to take another nice long walk, on which they would accompany them. It was a brand-new satisfaction they did not want to miss. After all, from a dog's standpoint, humans are made to take long walks with, among other things. The dogs greeted the people with tail-waggings and cordiality.

The dogs made a great difference in the adjustment of the tribe to life upon the plateau. Their friendship assured the new status of human life. Burl and his fellows had ceased to be fugitive game for any insect murderer. They had hoped to become unpursued foragers—because they could hardly imagine anything else. But when the dogs joined them, they were immediately raised to the estate of hunters. The men did not domesticate the dogs. They made friends with them. The dogs did not subjugate themselves to the men. They joined them—at first tentatively, and then with worshipful enthusiasm. And the partnership was so inevitably a right one that within a month it was as if it had always been.

Actually, save for a mere two thousand years, it had been.

At the end of a month the tribe had a permanent encampment. There were caves at a suitable distance from the slope up which most wanderers from the lowlands came. Cori's oldest child found the chrysalis of a giant butterfly, whose caterpillar form had so offensive an odor that the dogs had not attacked it. But when it emerged from the chrysalis, men and dogs together assailed it before it could take flight. They ended the enterprise with warm mutual approval. The humans had acquired great wings with which to make warm cloaks—very useful against the evening chill Dogs and men, alike, had feasted.

Then, one dawning, the dogs made a vast outcry which awoke the tribesmen. Burl led the rush to the spot. They did battle with a monster nocturnal beetle, less chilled than most such invaders. In the gray dawnlight Burl realized that the darting, yapping dogs kept the creature's full attention. He crippled, and then killed it with his spear. The feat appeared to earn him warm admiration from the dogs. Burl wore a moth's feathery antenna again, bound to his forehead like a knight's plumes. He looked very splendid.

The entire pattern of human life changed swiftly, as if

an entire revelation had been granted to men. The ground
was often thorny. One man pierced his foot. Old Tama,
scolding him for his carelessness, bound a strip of wing-fabric about it so he could walk. The injured foot was more
comfortable than the one still unhurt. Within a week the
women were busily contriving divers forms of footgear to
achieve greater comfort for everybody. One day Saya admired glistening red berries and tried to pluck one, and they
stained her fingers. She licked her fingers to clean them—
and berries were added to the tribe's menu. A veritable orgy
of experiment began, which is a state of things which is extremely rare in human affairs. A race with an established
culture and tradition does not abandon old ways of doing
things without profound reason. But men who have abandoned their old ways can discover astonishingly useful new
ones.

Already the dogs were established as sentries and
watchmen, and as friends to every member of the tribe. By
now mothers did not feel alarmed if a child wandered out of
sight. There would be dogs along. No danger could approach a child without vociferous warning from the dogs.
Men went hunting, now, with zestful tail-wagging dogs as
companions in the chase. Dor killed a torpid minotaur-bee-
tle alone, save for assisting dogs, and Burl felt a twinge of
jealousy. But then Burl, himself, battled a black male spider
in a lone duel—with dogs to help. By the time a stray monster from the lowlands reached this area, it was dazed and
half-numbed by one night of continuous chill. Even the
black spider could not find the energy to leap. It fought like
a fiend, yet sluggishly. Burl killed this one while the dogs
kept it busy—and the dogs were reproachful because he car-

ried it back to the tribal headquarters before dividing it
among his assistants. Afterward, he realized that though he
could have avoided the fight he would have been ashamed
to do so, while the dogs barked and snapped at its furry legs.

It was while things were in this state that the way of life
for human beings on the forgotten planet was settled for all
time. Burl and Saya went out early one morning with the
dogs, to hunt for meat for the village. Hunting was easiest in
the early hours, while creatures that strayed up the night before were still sluggish with cold. Often, hunting was merely
butchery of an enfeebled monster to whom any effort at all
was terribly difficult.

This morning they strode away briskly. The dogs roved
exuberantly through the brush before them. They were
some five miles from the village when the dogs bayed game.
And Burl and Saya ran to the spot with ready spears—which
was something of a change from their former actions on notice of a carnivore abroad. They found the dogs dancing and
barking around one of the most ferocious of the meat-eating
beetles. It was not unduly large, to be sure. Its body might
have been four feet long, or thereabouts. But its horrible
gaping mandibles added a good three feet more.

Those scythelike weapons gaped wide—opening sidewise as insects' jaws do—as the beetle snapped hideously at
its attackers, swinging about as the dogs dashed at it. Its legs
were spurred and spiked and armed with dagger-like spines.
Burl plunged into the fight.

The great mandibles clicked and clashed. They were
capable of disemboweling a man or snapping a dog's body
in half without effort. There were whistling noises as the
beetle breathed through its abdominal spiracles. It fought

furiously, making ferocious charges at the dogs who tormented and bewildered it. But they created the most zestfully excited of tumults.

Burl and Saya were, of course, at least as absorbed and excited as the dogs, or they would have noticed the thing that was to make so much difference to every human being, not only on the plateau but still down in the lowlands. This unnoticed thing was beyond their imagining. There had been nothing else like it on this world in many hundreds of years. It was half a dozen miles away and perhaps a thousand feet high when Burl and Saya prepared to intervene professionally on behalf of the dogs. It was a silvery needle, floating unsupported in the air. As they entered the battle, it swerved and moved swiftly in their direction.

It was silent, and they did not notice. They knew of no reason to scan the sky in daytime. And there was business on hand, anyhow.

Burl leaped in toward the beetle with a lance-thrust at the tough integument where an armored leg joined the creature's body. He missed, and the beetle whirled. Saya flashed her cloak before the monster so that it seemed a larger and a nearer antagonist. As the creature whirled again, Burl stabbed and a hind-leg crumpled.

Instantly the thing was limping. A beetle does not use its legs like four-legged creatures. A beetle moving shifts the two end legs on one side and the central leg on the other, so that it always stands on an adjustable tripod of limbs. It cannot adjust readily to crippling. A dog snatched at a spiny lower leg and crunched—and darted away. The machinelike monster uttered a formless, deep-bass cry and was spurred to unbelievable fierceness. The fight became a thing of furious

movement and joyous uproar, with Burl striking once at a
multiple eye so the pain would deflect it from a charge at
Saya, and Saya again deflecting it with her cloak and once
breathlessly trying to strike it with her shorter spear.

They struck it again, and a third time, and it sank horribly to the ground, all three legs on one side crippled. The
remaining three thrust and thrust and struggled senselessly—and suddenly it was on its back, still striking its gigantic jaws frantically in the hope of murder. But then Burl
struck home between two armor-plates where a ganglion was
almost exposed. The blow killed it instantly.

Burl and Saya were smiling at each other when there
was a monstrous sound of crashing trees. They whirled. The
dogs pricked up their ears. One of them barked defiantly.

Something huge—truly huge!—had settled to the
ground a bare two hundred yards away. It was metal, and
there were ports in its sides, and it was quite beyond imagining. Because, of course, no space-ship had landed on this
planet in forty-odd human generations.

A port opened as they stared at it. Men came out. Burl
and Saya were barbarically attired, but they had been fighting some sort of local monster—the men on the space-ship
could not quite grasp what they had seen—and they had
been helped by dogs. Human beings and dogs, together, always mean some sort of civilization.

The dogs gave an impression of a very high level indeed.
They trotted confidently over to the ship, and they sniffed
cautiously at the men who had landed. Then their behavior
was admirable. They greeted the new-come men with the
self-confident cordiality of dogs who are on the best possible
terms with human beings—and there was no question of

any suspicion by anybody The attitude of a man toward a dog is a perfectly valid indication of his character, if not of his technical education. And the newcomers knew how to treat dogs.

So Burl and Saya went forward, with the confident pleasure with which well-raised children and other persons of innate dignity greet strangers.

The ship was the *Wapiti*, a private cruiser doing incidental exploration for the Biological Survey in the course of a trip after good hunting. It had touched on the forgotten planet, and it would never be forgotten again.

Epilogue

THE SURVEY-SHIP *TETHYS* made the first landing on the forgotten planet, and the *Orana* followed, and some centuries later the *Ludred*. Then the planet was forgotten until the *Wapiti* arrived. The arrival of the *Wapiti* was as much an accident as the loss of the punched card which caused the planet to be overlooked for some thousands of years. Somebody had noticed that the sun around which it circled was of a type which usually has useful planets, but there was no record that it had ever been visited. So a request to the sportsmen on the *Wapiti* had caused them to turn aside. They considered, anyhow, that it would be interesting to land on a brand-new world or two. They considered it fascinating to find human beings there before them. But they could not understand the use of such primitive weapons or garments of such barbaric splendor. They had trouble, too, because in forty-odd generations the speech of the universe had changed, while Burl and Saya spoke a very archaic language indeed.

201

But there was an educator on the *Wapiti*. It was quite standard apparatus—simply basic-education for a human child, so that one's school-years could be begun with a backlog of correct speech, and reading, with the practical facts of mathematics, sanitation, and the general information that any human being anywhere needs to know. Children use it before they start school, and they absorb its information quite painlessly. It is rare that an adult needs it But Burl and Saya did.

Burl was politely invited to wear the head-set, and he politely obliged. He found himself equipped with a new language and what seemed to him an astonishing amount of information. Among the information was the item that he was going to have—as an adult—a severe headache. Which he did. Also included was the fact that the making of records for such educators was so laborious a process that it took generations to compile one master-record for the instruments.

Burl, with a splitting headache, nevertheless urged Saya to join him in getting an education. And she did. And thereafter they were able to converse with the sportsmen on the *Wapiti* comfortably enough—except for their headaches.

And all this led to extremely satisfactory arrangements. Sportsmen could not but be enthusiastic about the hunting of giant insects with dogs and spears. The sportsmen on the *Wapiti* wanted some of that kind of sport. Burl's fellow tribesmen were delighted to oblige—though they had not quite the zest of Burl. They had to acquire educations in their turn, so they could talk to their new hunting-companions. But the hunting was magnificent. The *Wapiti* abandoned its original plans and settled down for a stay.

Presently Burl's casual talk of the lowlands produced results. An atmosphere-flier came out of the ship's storage-compartments. And through the educator Burl was now a civilized man. He had not the specialized later information of his guests, but he had knowledge they could not dream of, and which it would take much of a century to put in recordable form for an educator.

So an atmosphere-flier went down into the lowlands through the cloud-banks. There were three men on board. They had good hunting. Magnificent hunting. Even more importantly, they found another cluster of human beings who lived as fugitives among the insect giants. They brought them to the plateau, a few at a time. Sportsmen stayed in the lowlands with modern weapons, hunting enthusiastically, while the transfer took place.

In all, the *Wapiti* stayed for two months Earthtime. When it left, its sportsmen had such trophies as would make them envied of all other hunters in three star-clusters. They left behind weapons and atmosphere-fliers and their library and tools. But they took with them enthusiasm for the sport on the once-forgotten planet, and rather warm feelings of friendship for Burl.

They sent their friends back. The next ship to come in found a small city on the plateau, with a population of three hundred souls—all civilized by educator. Naturally, they'd had no trouble building civilized dwellings or practising sanitation, or developing a neatly adapted culture-pattern for their particular environment. This second ship brought more weapons and fliers and news from the first party about commercial demand for the incredibly luxurious moth-fur, to be found on only one planet in all the galaxy.

The fourth ship to land on the plateau was a trading-ship, anxious to load such furs for recklessly bidding merchants in a dozen interplanetary marts. There were then nearly a thousand people living on the plateau. They had a natural monopoly—not of moth-fur and butterfly-wing fabric, and panels of irridescent chitin for luxurious decoration, but—of the strictly practical and detailed knowledge of insect-habits which made it possible to obtain them. Off-planet visitors who tried to hunt without local knowledge did not come back from the lowlands. In time, Burl firmly enacted a planetary law which forbade the inexperienced to go below the cloud-layer.

Because, of course, a government had to be formed for the planet. But men with the basic education of citizens everywhere did not fumble it. They had a job to do which was more important than anybody's vanity. It was a job which gave deep and abiding satisfaction. When naked, trembling folk were found in the mushroom-jungles and brought to the plateau, they had one instant, feverish desire as soon as they got over the headache from the educator.

They wanted to go back to the lowlands. It was profitable, to be sure. But it was even more of a satisfaction to hunt and kill the monsters that had hunted and killed men for so long. It felt good, too, to find other humans and bring them out to sunshine.

So nowadays the forgotten planet has ceased to be forgotten. It is hardly necessary to name it, because its name is known through all the Galaxy. Its population is not large, so far, but it is an interesting place to live in. In the popular mind, it is the most glamorous of all possible worlds—and for easily understandable reasons. The inhabitants of its capital city wear moth-fur garments and butterfly-wing cloaks for the benefit of their fellows in the lowlands. There is no day but fliers take off and dive down into the mists. When human hunters are in the lowlands, they dress as the lowlanders they used to be, so that lowlanders who may spy them will be sure that they are men, and friends, and come to them to be raised to proper dignity above the insects. It is not unusual for a man to be brought up to sunshine, and have his session with the educator, and be flying his own assigned atmosphere-flier within a week, diving back above what used to be the place where he was hunted, but where he has become the hunter.

It is a very pleasant arrangement. The search for more humans in the lowlands is a prosperous business, even when it is unsuccessful. The wings of white Morpho butterflies bring the highest prices, but even a common swallow-tail is riches, and the fur of caterpillars—duly processed—goes into the holds of the planet-owned space-line ships with the care given elsewhere to platinum and diamonds.

And also it is good sport. The planet is a sportsman's paradise. There are not too many visitors. Nobody may go hunting without an experienced host. And off-planet sportsmen tend to feel somewhat queasy after a session as guest of the folk who have made Burl their planet-president. Visitors are not so much alarmed at fighting flying beetles in mid-air, even though the beetles may compare with the hunters' craft in size and are terrifically tenacious of life. The thing that appalls strangers is the insistence of Burl's fellow-citizens—no longer only tribesmen—upon fighting spiders on the ground. With their memories, they like it that way. It's more satisfactory.

Not long ago the Planet President of Sumor XI was Burl's guest for a hunt. Sumor XI is a highly civilized planet, and life there has become tame. Its president is an ardent hunter. He liked Burl, who is still all hard muscle despite his graying hair. He and Saya have a very comfortable dwelling, and now that their children are grown they have room in it even for a planet president, if he comes as a sportsman guest. The Planet President of Sumor XI even liked the informal atmosphere of a house where pleasantly self-possessed dogs curl up comfortably on rugs of emperor-moth down that elsewhere are beyond price.

But the President of Sumor XI was embarrassed on his visit. He and Burl are both hunters, and they are highly congenial. But the President of Sumor XI was upset on his last flight to the lowlands. Burl got out of the atmosphere-flier alone, and for pure deep personal satisfaction he fought a mastodon-sized wolf spider with nothing but a spear.

He killed the creature, of course. But the President of Sumor XI was embarrassed. He wouldn't have dared try it. He felt that, however sporting it might be, it was too risky a thing for a Planet President to do.

But Saya took it for granted.

Author's Note

T HIS IS SOMETHING of an oddity among fiction-stories, because some of its characters may be met in person if you wish. Down at the nearest weed-patch or thicket you are quite likely to see a large and unusually perfect spider-web with a zig-zag ribbon woven into its center. Its engineer is the yellow-banded garden spider (*Epeira Fasciata*) whose abdomen may be as big as your thumb. I do not name it to impress you, but to suggest a sort of science-fiction experience.

Take a bit of straw and disturb the web. Don't break the cables. Simply tap them a little. The spider will know by the feel of things that you aren't prey and that it can't eat you. So it will set about frightening you away. It will run nimbly to the center of the web and shake itself violently. The whole web will vibrate, so that presently the spider may be swinging through an arc inches in length, and blurred by the speed of its swing. You are supposed to be scared. When you are alarmed enough, the spider will stop.

That spider, very much magnified, is in this book with crickets and grasshoppers and divers beetles you may not know personally. But this is not an insect-book, but science-fiction. If the habits of the creatures in it are authentic, it is because they are much more dramatic and interesting than things one can invent.

Since science-fiction does deal with matters that are more or less true, here is a list of other books written about some of the minor characters in this. I most earnestly suggest Fabre. The man was good!

A bibliography is usually a list of dull dry books placed at the end of a dull tedious book, assuring the reader that if he reads the listed books he will be more bored still. This is not that kind of bibliography. These books, while absolutely factual, are much more interesting than most fiction and can be read as if they were make-believe instead of the sound and honest work they are.

For anybody who finds the insects in this book interesting:

The Life of the Spider
The Life of the Fly
Social Life in the Insect World
The Bramblebees and Others
The Life of the Grasshopper
The Wonders of Instinct
The Mason-wasps

The Firefly and so on. These are by Jean Henri Fabre, who was not only a painstaking and meticulous scientific observer, but somebody whom you will consider your friend. His personality comes through and he was a most likeable person.

Edge of the Jungle, Ralph Beebe.
There is excellent material on the army ant in this book.
One can recommend his books without any exceptions that
I know of.

Life of the Bee, Maurice Maeterlinck.
This is, of course, a classic of literature.

Murray Leinster

"Ardudwy"
Gloucester, Va.

FINE SCIENCE FICTION AND
FANTASY TITLES AVAILABLE
FROM CARROLL & GRAF

☐ Pringle, David/SCIENCE FICTION: THE 100
  BEST NOVELS $7.95
☐ Siodmak, Curt/DONOVAN'S BRAIN $3.50
☐ Sladek, John/THE MULLER-FOKKER EFFECT $3.95
☐ Sladek, John/RODERICK $3.95
☐ Sladek, John/RODERICK AT RANDOM $3.95
☐ Stableford, Brian/THE WALKING SHADOW $3.95
☐ Stevens, Francis/CITADEL OF FEAR $3.50
☐ Stevens, Francis/CLAIMED $3.50
☐ Stevens, Francis/THE HEADS OF CERBERUS $3.50
☐ Stoker, Bram/THE JEWEL OF SEVEN STARS $3.95
☐ Sturgeon, Theodore/THE DREAMING
  JEWELS $3.95
☐ Sturgeon, Theodore/VENUS PLUS X $3.95
☐ Sturgeon, Theodore/THE GOLDEN HELIX $3.95
☐ Watson, Ian/CHEKHOV'S JOURNEY Cloth $16.95
☐ Watson, Ian/THE EMBEDDING $3.95
☐ Wolfe, Bernard/LIMBO $4.95

FINE MYSTERY AND SUSPENSE
TITLES FROM CARROLL & GRAF

- [ ] Bentley, E.C./TRENT'S OWN CASE $3.95
- [ ] Blake, Nicholas/MURDER WITH MALICE $3.95
- [ ] Blake, Nicholas/A TANGLED WEB $3.50
- [ ] Boucher, Anthony/THE CASE OF THE BAKER STREET IRREGULARS $3.95
- [ ] Boucher, Anthony (ed.)/FOUR AND TWENTY BLOODHOUNDS $3.95
- [ ] Brand, Christianna/DEATH IN HIGH HEELS $3.95
- [ ] Brand, Christianna/FOG OF DOUBT $3.50
- [ ] Brand, Christianna/TOUR DE FORCE $3.95
- [ ] Brown, Fredric/THE LENIENT BEAST $3.50
- [ ] Brown, Fredric/MURDER CAN BE FUN $3.95
- [ ] Brown, Fredric/THE SCREAMING MIMI $3.50
- [ ] Browne, Howard/THIN AIR $3.50
- [ ] Buchan, John/JOHN MACNAB $3.95
- [ ] Buchan, John/WITCH WOOD $3.95
- [ ] Burnett, W.R./LITTLE CAESAR $3.50
- [ ] Butler, Gerald/KISS THE BLOOD OFF MY HANDS $3.95
- [ ] Carr, John Dickson/THE BRIDE OF NEWGATE $3.95
- [ ] Carr, John Dickson/CAPTAIN CUT-THROAT $3.95
- [ ] Carr, John Dickson/DARK OF THE MOON $3.50
- [ ] Carr, John Dickson/DEADLY HALL $3.95
- [ ] Carr, John Dickson/DEMONIACS $3.95
- [ ] Carr, John Dickson/THE DEVIL IN VELVET $3.95
- [ ] Carr, John Dickson/THE EMPEROR'S SNUFF-BOX $3.50
- [ ] Carr, John Dickson/FIRE, BURN! $3.50
- [ ] Carr, John Dickson/IN SPITE OF THUNDER $3.50
- [ ] Carr, John Dickson/LOST GALLOWS $3.50
- [ ] Carr, John Dickson/MOST SECRET $3.95
- [ ] Carr, John Dickson/NINE WRONG ANSWERS $3.50
- [ ] Carr, John Dickson/PAPA LA-BAS $3.95

- [ ] Chesterton, G.K./THE CLUB OF QUEER TRADES $3.95
- [ ] Chesterton, G. K./THE MAN WHO KNEW TOO MUCH $3.95
- [ ] Chesterton, G. K./THE MAN WHO WAS THURSDAY $3.50
- [ ] Coles, Manning/ALL THAT GLITTERS $3.95
- [ ] Coles, Manning/THE FIFTH MAN $2.95
- [ ] Coles, Manning/GREEN HAZARD $3.95
- [ ] Coles, Manning/THE MAN IN THE GREEN HAT $3.50
- [ ] Coles, Manning/NO ENTRY $3.50
- [ ] Collins, Michael/WALK A BLACK WIND $3.95
- [ ] Crofts, Freeman Wills/THE CASK $3.95
- [ ] Crofts, Freeman Wills/INSPECTOR FRENCH'S GREATEST CASE $3.50
- [ ] Dewey, Thomas B./THE BRAVE, BAD GIRLS $3.50
- [ ] Dewey, Thomas B./DEADLINE $3.50
- [ ] Dewey, Thomas B./THE MEAN STREETS $3.50
- [ ] Dickson, Carter/THE CURSE OF THE BRONZE LAMP $3.50
- [ ] Disch, Thomas M & Sladek, John/ BLACK ALICE $3.95
- [ ] Du Maurier, Daphne/THE SCAPEGOAT $4.50
- [ ] Eberhart, Mignon/MESSAGE FROM HONG KONG $3.50
- [ ] Eastlake, William/CASTLE KEEP $3.50
- [ ] Fennelly, Tony/THE CLOSET HANGING $3.50
- [ ] Fennelly, Tony/THE GLORY HOLE MURDERS $2.95
- [ ] Freeman, R. Austin/THE EYE OF OSIRIS $3.95
- [ ] Freeman, R. Austin/MYSTERY OF ANGELINA FROOD $3.95
- [ ] Freeman, R. Austin/THE RED THUMB MARK $3.50
- [ ] Gilbert, Michael/THE DOORS OPEN $3.95
- [ ] Gilbert, Michael/GAME WITHOUT RULES $3.95
- [ ] Gilbert, Michael/THE 92nd TIGER $3.95
- [ ] Gilbert, Michael/OVERDRIVE $3.95
- [ ] Graham, Winston/MARNIE $3.95
- [ ] Greeley, Andrew/DEATH IN APRIL $3.95
- [ ] Hornung, E.W./THE AMATEUR CRACKSMAN $3.95
- [ ] Hughes, Dorothy B./THE EXPENDABLE MAN $3.50

☐ Hughes, Dorothy B./THE FALLEN SPARROW		$3.50
☐ Hughes, Dorothy B./IN A LONELY PLACE		$3.50
☐ Hughes, Dorothy B./RIDE THE PINK HORSE		$3.95
☐ Innes, Hammond/ATLANTIC FURY		$3.50
☐ Innes, Hammond/THE LAND GOD GAVE TO CAIN		$3.50
☐ Kitchin, C. H. B./DEATH OF HIS UNCLE		$3.95
☐ Kitchin, C. H. B./DEATH OF MY AUNT		$3.50
☐ L'Amour, Louis/THE HILLS OF HOMICIDE		$2.95
☐ Lewis, Norman/THE MAN IN THE MIDDLE		$3.50
☐ MacDonald, John D./TWO		$2.50
☐ MacDonald, Philip/THE RASP		$3.50
☐ Mason, A.E.W./AT THE VILLA ROSE		$3.50
☐ Mason, A.E.W./THE HOUSE OF THE ARROW		$3.50
☐ Priestley, J.B./SALT IS LEAVING		$3.95
☐ Queen, Ellery/THE FINISHING STROKE		$3.95
☐ Rogers, Joel T./THE RED RIGHT HAND		$3.50
☐ 'Sapper'/BULLDOG DRUMMOND		$3.50
☐ Siodmak, Curt/DONOVAN'S BRAIN		$3.50
☐ Symons, Julian/BLAND BEGINNING		$3.95
☐ Symons, Julian/BOGUE'S FORTUNE		$3.95
☐ Symons, Julian/THE BROKEN PENNY		$3.95
☐ Wainwright, John/ALL ON A SUMMER'S DAY		$3.50
☐ Wallace, Edgar/THE FOUR JUST MEN		$2.95
☐ Waugh, Hillary/SLEEP LONG, MY LOVE		$3.95
☐ Willeford, Charles/THE WOMAN CHASER		$3.95

Available from fine bookstores everywhere or use this coupon for ordering.

Carroll & Graf Publishers, Inc., 260 Fifth Avenue, N.Y., N.Y. 10001

Please send me the books I have checked above. I am enclosing
$_____ (please add $1.00 per title to cover postage and
handling.) Send check or money order—no cash or C.O.D.'s
please. N.Y. residents please add 8¼% sales tax.

Mr/Mrs/Ms _____

Address _____

City _____ State/Zip _____

Please allow four to six weeks for delivery.